G.O.R.E SECTOR
BOOK 2

COLUBER

A NOVEL BY MICHAEL COLE

SEVEREDPRESS

COLUBER

Copyright © 2024 by MICHAEL COLE

WWW.SEVEREDPRESS.COM

All rights reserved. No part of this book may be reproduced or transmitted in any form or by any electronic or mechanical means, including photocopying, recording or by any information and retrieval system, without the written permission of the publisher and author, except where permitted by law.

This novel is a work of fiction. Names, characters, places and incidents are the product of the author's imagination, or are used fictitiously. Any resemblance to actual events, locales or persons, living or dead, is purely coincidental.

ISBN: 978-1-923165-23-6

CHAPTER 1

"Falcon, you in position?"

"Almost there, Captain. What's your rush? Got a date?"

"No time. Not with our schedule. That said, I'd like to wrap this up. Eagle Squadron, take position on the east side."

"This is General Kilmore. Eagle One, I want some of your choppers holding at a seven-hundred-yard perimeter. If any bugs try to make a run for it, they're all yours."

"Eagle One here. Copy that, General. Eagle Seven, Eight, and Nine are taking position to seven hundred yards."

"Eagle One, I want the rest of your aircraft to maintain a distance of one hundred meters from the target."

"Copy that. Fellas, you heard the Captain."

"Dr. Tate, how're your rovers looking?"

"Getting them ready, Captain. We're about to get this party started."

Corporal Mace Lamont chuckled as he listened to the radio chatter. As usual, Raptor Pack did not fail to amuse with their back-and-forths, whether it was in person or over the radio. More importantly, their reconnaissance proved successful in locating the next hornet nest.

In the cleanup effort following the battle against the wasp and hornet hives in Ramsey County, Oregon, came a horrifying discovery. Two hornet egg casings, identical to Dr. Charity Black's descriptions of queen hornets' eggs, were discovered. With none of the insect bodies matching the description of hornet princesses, G.O.R.E.

Sector could only make one conclusion: Two princesses had escaped before the destruction of their colony.

Raptor Pack was already responding to an incident in the Everglades, in which a giant mutated catfish was terrorizing a small fishing village. Once that threat had been dealt with, they moved straight to tracking the whereabouts of the missing princesses.

The first had been located in Texas. Thanks to Howard Tate wisely positioning surveillance satellites over the Ramsey County battlegrounds, Raptor Pack was able to track their flightpaths with relative ease. The one in Texas was quickly destroyed while it was in the beginning stages of forming its nest.

The second one migrated several miles north, ultimately settling in the rolling hills of Wyoming. Unlike her sister, this queen managed to establish a young colony, which had quickly gone to work attacking nearby ranches. So far, it appeared that livestock and wildlife was this colony's only victims. If it wasn't eradicated immediately, their palate would surely expand.

Corporal Lamont, an Army veteran of four years, wished he could play a part in the fun. The hive was three miles southeast, across a winding river which stretched across the landscape. The other two members of his scout team felt the same. Alas, they would have to wait for another day to shoot monsters. Thanks to the Ecclesiastes Intergalactic Meteor storm of 2019, they would surely get another change.

For now, Scout Team Four was on the lookout for tunnels.

"Sun's up," Private John Cagle said, nodding to the east.

The third member of the scout team, Private Glen Furst, shivered. "'Bout damn time. You'd think these bugs would've picked a warmer state, like Arizona or California."

Lamont pivoted to his left and shot a glare at the twenty-three-year-old soldier. "Oh, for crying out loud! It's summer. Not that cold at all."

"He's from Texas, Corporal," Cagle said with a chuckle. "Anything that isn't a hundred thousand degrees he considers ice-cold."

Lamont sniggered. "Your school district probably closed whenever they got a thin coating of snow in the winter."

"Jealous?" Furst said.

The Corporal sported a grin and tilted his head to the northwest. "Come on. Let's keep going. We're not here for chit chat. Raptor Pack said there's a few properties around this area. We need to make sure they evacuated. And keep an eye out for any oddities in the land. Dr. Black said this colony of hornets have a variation in their mutation, which causes them to dig vast tunnels underground. Maybe they wish they were ants, I don't know. Regardless, keep your eyes peeled. We don't want them escaping the hellfire G.O.R.E. Sector is about to rain down on them."

"We're three miles away. At least," Cagle said. "I highly doubt those bugs had enough time, or motivation, to dig all the way out…" His voice trailed off and his gaze shifted to the north. He hustled several yards, stopping by a towering Douglas fir tree. "Okay, maybe I spoke too soon."

"Got something?" Lamont asked.

Cagle nodded. "Looks like it."

"Ah, you beat me to it," Private Furst said, hustling over to his position. True to the pronunciation of his name, the soldier was eager to be first to accomplish every task assigned to the team. First to shoot something, first to find any clues, first to dig into the chow, and so forth. In this case, he hoped to be first to find any signs of underground tunneling.

Lamont was right behind him. He passed a few smaller trees and ascended the small mound of earth surrounding the base of the Douglas fir. On the other side was the gaping mouth of a very large underground passageway. Lamont aimed a flashlight into the tunnel. Its walls were relatively smooth, spaced out at nearly seven feet. Twelve feet down was a bend, leading to a much larger section which appeared to be heading northeast.

"Can't believe they've dug this far already," Cagle said.

"Hold up," Lamont said. "Are we sure this is from the hornets? Raptor Pack found tunnels near the hive, and they were no bigger than four feet in width. This is maybe six or seven." He stood over the entrance, studying it with a nervous gaze. He turned his head over his right shoulder…to the southeast, where the hive was located. The tunnel bend was heading *north.* Away from the nest. "This can't be right. I'm not sure this is related to the situation at hand."

Cagle shrugged. "What else could it be, Corporal? Unless there's a giant mole digging around out here, I think it's safe to assume this thing is related to the hornet nest."

"Have you seen some of the weird stuff that's popped up since the meteor storm?" Furst said. "A giant mole wouldn't necessarily be out of the question."

"Alright, let's cut the chatter," Lamont said. "Furst, get the marker out of your pack. If you want to be 'first' to do something today, be the first to set up a GPS marker and tripwire. I don't want anything escaping through this tunnel."

"You got it, sir," Furst replied. He placed his pack on the ground and removed a small tracking post and a few explosive charges. The tracking post was staked into the ground a few yards from the tunnel. An antennae extended from its top, blinking a red light. The location was marked.

Next, the soldier went to work planting explosives to the tunnel walls. Four blocks of C4 were activated and armed with a laser tripwire, which would trigger the explosives should anything attempt to come out.

Lamont stepped away and unclipped his radio from his vest. "Scout Four to Raptor Pack?"

"Captain Rodney here. Go ahead, Four."

"Sir, I wanted to inform you we've located a tunnel entrance roughly three miles northwest of the river cove, where we parked our patrol vehicle. I had Furst mark the location in case Dr. Black wants to look at it."

There was a brief moment of radio silence, during which the Captain was probably managing the current operation.

"Copy that, Four. We'll be over to take a look at it once this party is over."

Lamont smiled. "Understood, sir. Looking forward to listening to the fireworks from here."

"Sorry to say, our method of attack will involve something a lot quieter. I'll tell you about it later. Keep me posted on any updates. Rodney out."

Lamont slipped his radio into a slot in his vest, then turned to face Furst. The soldier stood up from the tunnel entrance and brushed his hands against his fatigues.

"Okay. Ready to go," he said. "If anything comes through here, it'll be in for a surprise."

"Time will tell," Lamont said. He gripped his rifle and casually walked north. "Let's move this way. I want to see if this tunnel comes out anywhere else."

"Corporal, it probably leads back to the nest," Cagle said. "Just because those bugs dig tunnels, it doesn't mean they always go in a straight line. Maybe one dug this far and decided to make a left turn at some point."

"*Or*...it could be something else," Furst said. "Maybe some of those big wasps, with a similar variation in their mutation. Or maybe a really fat princess hornet, spawned from the new colony. Whatever the case, I'd like to get first crack at those bad boys. I was at the Ridge in Oregon. The wasps killed many good men that day. The hornets would have done the same had we not stopped them first."

Cagle and Lamont nodded. All three of them were there, though in different places. Cagle was part of the town defense effort, which had also suffered heavy casualties when the wasp queen and her horde attacked. Corporal Lamont was on the ridge with Raptor Pack, having witnessed the death of the then-team leader Jacob Coltrane.

The emergence of those insects was the worst threat since the fall of the Ecclesiastes Intergalactic Meteor storm so far. Their appearance had shaken the entire planet, who was now aware of the existence of massive and deadly mutations. Only the existence of G.O.R.E. Sector, run by General Austin Kilmore, kept the world's population *somewhat* at ease.

Every threat level was different, but as recent events taught them, some could potentially lead to the extinction of the human race. Not one was benevolent. Perhaps the particles from the meteor storm corrupted the brain as well as the body. Or, they were forged out of pure evil, possessing the souls of anything it touched.

At this point, Lamont wasn't ready to rule anything out.

"Let's move."

With great enthusiasm, Furst unslung his weapon and took point. They went north, following the tunnel's projected route.

They crossed a few hundred yards of sparse forest, during which Furst began talking about some stupid cookout story with his ex-girlfriend's family. Corporal Lamont and Cagle repeatedly exchanged glances, seemingly using telepathy in an attempt to get the other to shut the idiot up. Ultimately, Lamont realized he would have to pull rank and order Furst to shut up about the vegan burgers.

As it turned out, he didn't have to, for Furst's story abruptly ended with a flabbergasted "Whoa."

They arrived at the peak of a tall hill overlooking a private property. A few trees obscured the view, but through the grove, they were still able to make out the view of an overturned pickup truck between a large cabin and a pond.

In the blink of an eye, the team was alert. Guns were shouldered, the muzzles sweeping the surrounding area. With no threat in sight, the team hurried down the hill, pausing every few yards to check for any movement.

After twenty yards, the ground leveled out. After forty yards, they arrived at the edge of the property. It was here where they realized the full extent of whatever disaster had befallen this place.

The cabin, originally a two-story structure, resembled a crushed soda can. The walls had been compressed into its center, the logs comprising them snapped like toothpicks. The roof had exploded outward like an over-compressed balloon, spewing wood and shingles onto the lawn. All around the cabin, the grass was marred by the trail of what must have been a large, yet narrow object. Looking at it, Lamont pictured the tire of a humongous monster truck rolling across the yard. Except this trail had no treads. And it was thirty times bigger. All he could see was flattened or uprooted grass.

Cagle went to the cabin and found the front door. It had literally popped off of its hinges. He peeked inside, then looked at the Corporal, shaking his head.

"If anyone survived this, they'll need an entire construction crew to get them out."

Lamont's eyes were frozen on the wreckage. "The bugs couldn't have done this. They rip things apart. This cabin looks like it has been… squeezed." He turned his eyes to the pickup truck. The windshield was smashed, the hood was crumpled, and the front left wheel had broken off entirely. Unlike the cabin, it had not been crushed, but by the looks of it, *tossed.*

The Corporal found himself turning a full three-sixty degrees. He was now suspicious of every square inch of forest that surrounded him. Though not as thick as the forests in Oregon where the wasp hive was discovered, it was still enough to obscure the view of enemies.

Private Furst completed a walk around the edge of the property line, shrugging as he rejoined his teammates.

"Nothing. Nobody's in sight. No sign of what did this, either."

"Son of a bitch." Lamont exhaled slowly. "That's what I get for thinking we'd be out of here in time for breakfast." He reached for his radio, intent on informing Raptor Pack of the situation.

All eyes turned to the sound of a faint *boom* echoing from the south. A tremor rippled under their boots. Lamont's blood rushed, creating an odd mix of dread and excitement.

"I think it's safe to assume those weren't hellfire missiles," Cagle said.

"Nope. Captain Rodney indicated they were trying to avoid use of explosives," Lamont said. "No, that was closer. Looks like something triggered the C4 we planted."

Without hesitation, Scout Team Four raced back the way they originally came, crossing the same hill and section of forest. Only this time, they were running. And did not have to endure Furst's storytelling along the way.

As they neared the tunnel, they were hit with an array of odors reminiscent of motor oil and pentaerythritol tetranitrate, which vaguely resembled burnt almonds. The C4 had indeed exploded.

"There it is," Cagle said.

Lamont saw it. The blast had nearly doubled the width of the entrance, which was now surrounded by a ring of hot dirt. The squad reduced their speed and approached with caution. Through the smoke, they searched for a corpse, or at least pieces of one. To their surprise, all they could see was dirt and grass. The tracking post was intact, having been placed outside the blast radius.

Shifting his gaze in every direction, Lamont confirmed there was no corpse in sight. If one existed, it was resting in the bend of the tunnel.

"Furst, take position three-o'clock of the entrance. Cagle, you go left, ten o'clock. Create a crossfire if anything comes out."

"You taking a look?" Furst asked. Lamont nodded. "All you're likely to see are pieces."

"Let's hope that's the case," Lamont replied.

He waited for his men to take position before approaching the tunnel. Boots imprinted on soft, warm soil as he neared its edge. Images of the cabin flashed in his mind's eye. There was no doubt it was related to the existence of whatever carved this underground channel. It was no wasp, that much was for certain. Hopefully, the next certainty would be its death.

He leaned over the edge and aimed a light into the bend.

"You've got to be kidding me."

"What?" Furst asked. "Is it big? Ugly? Huge?" He chuckled. "What did we kill?"

Lamont shook his head. "Nothing."

Furst squinted. "Heh?"

"There's nothing down here."

"Bull!" Cagle jogged to the tunnel and aimed his own flashlight inside. All he could see was dirt. "The remains must have fallen farther back to where we can't see."

"Maybe," Lamont said. "That, or its remains got tossed far and wide. Though, if that were the case, we should've seen something by now—" He turned around to search for any smoldering remains, instead taking notice of a strange groove in the soil. It was easy to miss, especially with the smoke fogging the air, but there all the same.

Cagle saw it too. "What is that?"

"It's the same kind of trail as we saw on the cabin yard," Lamont said.

The strange trail extended from the tunnel and went southwest, leaving flattened grass and some crushed vegetation in its wake. Its width was almost equal to that of the tunnel. What really concerned Lamont was the heavy realization that this trail was not present before. That fact led to a second realization: whatever emerged from the earth had survived the blast and was roaming free nearby.

Lamont pointed his rifle at the trees. "Keep your heads on a swivel, gentlemen. We're not alone out here."

"It could be anywhere by now," Furst said.

Cagle inched eastward, his weapon pointed at the trail. "We should head back to the IFAV."

Lamont gave thought to the suggestion, ultimately deciding his fellow soldier was right. Considering the threat was as yet unidentified and was proven to be resilient to C4 explosives, staying here was strictly suicide.

"I agree. Let's go."

"No argument here!" As Furst spoke, he was spinning on his heel and double-timing it to their vehicle. Consistent with his nature, Furst was first to get the hell out of dodge when things weren't in his team's favor.

Lamont and Cagle were a few yards behind him, the former glancing over his shoulder every few seconds to ensure that *thing* was not pursuing them.

After two minutes of travel, they could see the splashing of a small waterfall on the river. It was just a few dozen yards ahead.

By now, they were less than fifty feet from the riverside. The interim fast attack vehicle, generally referred as an IFAV, was in plain sight. Furst was already in the driver's seat. He started up the engine and gave his teammates a 'what's taking so long?' look.

Normally, Lamont would roast him for being such a wuss. In this case, however, he was glad to see his ride started up and ready to go.

His sense of relief was swiftly eradicated by a faint, but heart-stopping vibration under his feet. He came to a stop and threw his left arm out to halt Cagle. The soldier turned to question the Corporal, but then lowered his eyes to the earth after sensing the same tremor.

It was not a shockwave from any blasting. This tremor was isolated and moving in a very precise pattern.

The two men shared a glance. And a thought.

Something's moving beneath us.

It was at this point Lamont had one final realization. That trail he saw near the tunnel—the creature was not exiting when it triggered the C4, but rather *entering.*

The vibration continued past them, all the way to the IFAV. Furst glared at the men, unsure why they had stopped all of a sudden. He threw his hands out, ready to ask them what the problem was. Before the words came out, he got his answer.

A tremendous force came up from the earth, striking the vehicle from underneath. The IFAV was airborne and in a spiral, its occupant thrown from the driver's seat.

Furst hit the ground thirty feet from the shoreline, the vehicle striking down a few yards to his right. Its passenger side caved in on itself, generating a slew of sparks which sprayed onto a stream of spilt gasoline.

BOOM!

The IFAV went up in flames, instantly producing a thick wall of smoke.

Lamont and Cagle backed away, their weapons at the ready. Behind that thick wall of smoke was the meteor storm's latest abomination.

Furst was still alive. Despite being dazed, he managed to roll away from the burning vehicle. He managed to get on his hands and knees, ready to sprint into the forest.

He froze, sensing a presence bearing down on him. Against his better judgement, he peeked over his right shoulder, then screamed upon making eye contact with the demonic entity staring back at him.

Today, he was the first to die.

His screams were cut short by the snapping of jaws and the crunching of bone, preceding a wet slurping sound as he was slipped through the creature's long neck.

Lamont and Cagle unleashed their magazines. Bullets struck the rough, leathery flesh. The beast shook its head as though mildly annoyed, then coiled behind the smoke cloud, its serpentine shape a mere silhouette.

Until it struck.

Lamont found himself staring at the sky. He didn't even register getting knocked to the ground for a few long moments. His memory of the last few seconds were reduced to a single instance of the creature's neck lashing his torso as it bent to grab his partner.

More vibrations swept underneath him, this time originating from the writhing motion of a long, winding body. Tilting his head to his left, Lamont watched the legs of Private Cagle point skyward, gradually slipping between a mammoth set of jaws. The feet continued to twitch while throat muscles delivered him down a deep, dark tunnel. A small bulge formed on its throat, quickly traveling down its length until eventually vanishing.

The jaws closed and the head turned toward the Corporal. It reared back, ready to lash at its third target.

Lamont did not move. What was the point? Escape was impossible. All he could hope to do was warn Raptor Pack.

He snatched his radio and brought it to his lips. "Raptor Pack! By the river, there's a—"

SNAP!

Darkness enveloped him.

Death came a little later.

CHAPTER 2

"No rest for the weary."

When Captain Thomas Rodney accepted the job as the leader of Raptor Pack, he had no illusions of a laid-back, slow-paced career. His job orientation was second to none: saving the world from colonies of killer hornets and wasps. Mutated by alien particles that had rained down on Earth a few short years ago, they had morphed into a hyperviolent and invasive species. Had they not been wiped out by the brave men and women of G.O.R.E. Sector, the entire nation, and in time, the world at large would have been threatened.

The escape of two hornet queens and the formations of their hives hammered home this fact. Thomas' team quickly tracked down the first queen to a rural area in Texas, where it was in the early stages of forming a colony. Only a few worker hornets had been born, though an examination of the remains proved that hundreds of eggs had already been lain. Had the team arrived a day later, the swarm would have already dominated the entire county and would have forced evacuations for hundreds of miles.

It was in Badger County, Wyoming, where the second queen made her landing. It was an area of rolling hills and montane forests, mainly consisting of fir trees and ponderosa pines.

Thomas Rodney felt the wind in his hair as he gazed down from the open fuselage of the *Falcon-One-Five.* With Renee Larson at the controls, he had a bird's eye view of the nest and the G.O.R.E. Sector forces surrounding it.

The hill where the queen had dug in now resembled a miniature volcano, with a twelve-foot-wide opening at its top. What he and his team found more disturbing were the appearances of smaller openings found around the nest. They were no bigger than four feet in diameter, but proved more than enough to provide passage for the warrior hornets. Each known entrance had been marked with smoke, giving the Captain a visual of their locations. Four red clouds between the trees like tornados from hell.

"Captain, we've got another one," Charity Black said through his receiver. A few moments later, Thomas saw a fifth plume of smoke rising from the west end of the kill zone. It was roughly two hundred feet from the main entrance. A few rifle shots echoed from that direction. In that moment, Thomas caught a glimpse of a black shape zipping above the treetops. It vanished as quickly as it appeared, the gunfire having ceased.

"You okay over there, Doctor?" he asked.

"Yep. A couple of bouncers tried to pick a fight with us. I shot 'em, though," Charity said. Following her reply came a distinctly gruff and masculine clearing of the throat. Thomas grinned, imagining a pair of eyes boring into Charity Black, insisting she reveal a little detail she left out. *"Okay, alright, fine. I shot AT them. Archer MAY have made the kill shots."*

Thomas chuckled at that. "Ya missed, huh? I guess we shouldn't be too surprised. I mean, it's par for the course when it comes to Air Force people and all." His smile widened as he envisioned Charity's face turning beet red at that comment. A few other personnel went ahead and pressed their transmitters, letting their laughs be heard through the channel.

"Ohhhh… Funny, funny, funny, Captain… Archer, get that stupid grin off your face!" Charity said. *"Renee, if*

you were to tilt that bird a little more to port, I'd understand."

Just for fun, the pilot began to angle the *Falcon* to port, as though to let the Captain fall out.

"I could, but it won't do any good. He's harnessed in," she replied.

"Nice try," Thomas said. "Well done, Archer. Continue keeping the Doc in one piece. Lord knows she can't do it herself."

"Will do, Captain," the sniper replied.

"Oh, ha ha."

Renee gently steered the *Falcon* in a semi-circle, maintaining a safe distance from the hive's main entrance.

"So much for finishing this without firing a shot," she said.

Thomas shrugged. "If that's the only shooting that occurs today, I'll consider that a win."

He shifted his binocs back to the main entrance, then at the numerous helicopters surrounding the area. They were all in position, ready for a battle they would hopefully not have to fight. God willing, the team's new plan would wipe out the insects without a single one of them escaping the hive. Thomas was banking hard on the plan working. The last thing anyone wanted was a repeat of the last major insect encounter.

The Battle of Ramsey County, though ultimately successful, was a near-disaster. Many soldiers paid the ultimate sacrifice that day. In addition, the world was now aware of the existence of monsters and the organization created to fight it.

G.O.R.E. Sector, Giant Organism Reconnaissance and Extermination, continued to be front page news. Talking heads, both corporate and independent, spouted off their theories and opinions regarding the Sector. As more people learned of the danger the wasp colony posed, G.O.R.E. Sector faced increased skepticism. Many expressed disdain for the secrecy surrounding the agency, though some credited General Austin Kilmore for coming forward with the truth in a press conference. Despite receiving a verbal bombardment from Congress as a result, he remained in command of the Sector. Whilst much of the public was skeptical, many recognized G.O.R.E. Sector had prevented a catastrophic event. Removing General Kilmore would only serve to spark more outrage.

Thomas turned his glasses to the southernmost smoke trail. A hundred feet beyond it was a large hilltop swarming with vehicles and soldiers. Snipers took position everywhere, each one targeting one of the entrances with intent to blast any bug attempting to escape.

In the center of the gathering was a small tarpaulin canopy, casting shade over a folding desk. There, Dr. Howard Tate worked with a set of laptops linked to a control module. The morning sun glinted off two metal devices on his left. Rovers, visually similar to those used for lunar missions, were being prepped for the operation.

Standing nearby was General Austin Kilmore, supervising the operation with his own set of binoculars. A veteran of wars against human and mutant groups, he supported Thomas' proposed method of attack.

"Dr. Tate's just about ready, Captain," he said. *"Dr. Black, have you completed your scan of the nest's interior?"*

"That's affirmative, sir," Charity replied. *"Archer and I are on our way back to you. I'm uploading the data so you can view it on your tablets."*

An M1161 Growler emerged from the forest and parked near some Humvees on the west side of the hill. Thomas watched as Charity Black and Archer exited the vehicle and joined Howard and General Kilmore.

Thomas lowered his binocs and pulled a tablet from a large pocket on his vest. In that moment, he received the *ping* of Charity's file upload. He tapped on the document, bringing a digital map of the nest onto the screen.

"Whoa."

The nest was far deeper than he anticipated. Not only that, but it was structured a little differently than the last nests they had dealt with. The central entrance led to a tunnel which traveled straight down thirty feet, connecting to the main body of the nest.

Unlike the other nests, which mainly comprised of a typical honeycomb shape under the ground, this one had more of an hourglass figure. It was comprised of two chambers, stacked vertically and connected by a fairly small passageway. The first chamber was the larger of the two by a fourth. Like arms extending from an octopus, a series of tunnels protruded from the two sections, some of which continued on for several hundred yards.

"Captain? Did you receive the scan?" Charity asked.

"Ten-four," he replied. "Son of a bitch, they were really intricate when building this one, weren't they?"

"I'd say so. From what it seems, they're pretty closely related to the black hornets we dealt with in Oregon. As I mentioned before, it appears this group has slightly different characteristics."

"No kidding. They wish they were ants, apparently," Renee quipped.

"Maybe. But one thing's for sure: momma's been busy. I can guarantee you that top chamber is filled with eggs and larvae. The queen is probably in the bottom chamber. Aside from the little connector tunnel, she's got over forty feet of earth shielding her from anything we do to the top section."

Thomas inhaled deeply, the magnitude of the situation weighing heavier on his shoulders with each passing moment.

"Dr. Tate? How confident are you that your pesticides can kill that queen?"

"If I can get one of my rovers down there, extremely. We managed to test a sample on a drone we captured in Texas. Worked like a charm. The bad boys in this nest may have different engineering tastes, but their biology should be more or less the same."

"Do you have enough of it?"

"Um…"

'Um'. Never what anyone wanted to hear in a situation like this.

"…Yeah, I think so. I have three rovers. One of the tunnels runs deep. I can get one in the top chamber and one in the second. Both have enough pesticide to fill that area."

For a moment, Thomas was relieved.

"There is one little catch."

That relief was instantly wiped away.

"And that is?"

"The drones will definitely detect the rovers as they're entering the nest and go on the attack. I was hoping by the time we arrived that the nest would not be so large, and that there'd only be a few hornet offspring like the last one. Now, I have three rovers, so we have some margin of error. But, even so, anything that approaches the nest will be swarmed."

"Here's an idea," Renee called from the cockpit. "What if I brought us in close to the center opening? We can drop a couple of cannisters from where you're standing. Probably kill most of them before they can escape."

Thomas thought about it for a moment, then shook his head. "No. We're pushing our luck as it is. To drop that thing in, we'd have to get pretty damn close. We already came within seventy feet of it, and a bunch of hornets emerged through the mound. We'd have to get closer than that to get the cannister inside."

"I can do it, Captain. We can drop it in, and I'll gun the engines, and—"

"No, Renee." Thomas watched the activity on the mound. Though he would not admit it, he could not determine which tactic was best suited to get the job done.

A few moments of silence passed before General Kilmore entered the conversation.

"Delaying will only allow the enemy time to increase their numbers. They haven't killed anyone yet. In twenty-four hours, that will certainly change. This is your operation, Captain. Your team, your call. But you will need to make one, and fast."

Thomas stood silent with a contemptuous gaze burning into the image. Just the sight of the layout was frustrating. It was as though the bugs had anticipated their attack and had constructed their fortress accordingly. If the chemical attack did not work, the choppers would have no choice but to resort to the old-school method of blasting the hell out of the thing. Considering the amount of dirt and rock in-between, it would take an incredible amount of firepower just to destroy the upper chamber. Accomplishing the objective without unleashing God-knows how many hornets would be impossible. A dogfight would ensue. Many soldiers would die. And planning an alternative strategy would take too long.

They needed to destroy this thing now.

Thomas took a few glances at the units in the surrounding area, ultimately settling on his teammates on the hillside. He had promised Jacob Coltrane, the former leader of Raptor Pack, that he would keep his team alive. It was not a promise he made lightly. Though they only worked together for a short time, Thomas considered his team as family. With his wife gone, they were the only family he had on this earth.

The most likely method of accomplishing the objective and keeping that promise was to gas the nest. If only there was a way to get the rover inside without the bugs disabling it.

He thought of the battle against the wasp hive and the drastic measures they pulled off to kill the queen. Her hide was thick enough to withstand missile strikes. Only quick thinking, fast acting, and some luck allowed them to pull off a win. In the end, they used hornet pheromones to get the queen's own guards to attack her. In the attempt, Renee and Archer were nearly killed. Had Howard's drones arrived with the pheromones five seconds later, they would have been.

Thomas was not keen on playing with their lives. Had it not been for Raptor Pack and G.O.R.E. Sector, he would have lost his. Still working as a deputy sheriff for Ramsey County, he investigated a string of mysterious disappearances, only to come face-to-face with a swarm of deadly hornets. His fellow deputies had been stung to death, with Thomas moments away from the same fate when Raptor Pack showed up.

That following morning, Jacob Coltrane paid the ultimate sacrifice. His final words to Thomas were ones of dedication and leadership.

'It's your turn now. Thomas… save them. Save my team. Save the world.'

His reminiscing sparked a new idea.

"Pheromones."

"Beg your pardon, Captain?" Renee said. "Listen, we work well together and all… and I can't blame you for getting the hots after seeing yours truly in action. But…"

"Oh, shut up, Ensign," Thomas said. "I'm talking about the bugs. Howard, Charity. You guys shot down a couple of drones near the west entrance."

"Correct," Charity said.

"Well, if we're being precise, Archer shot 'em," Howard added.

"Oh, bite me. Anyway, what do you have in mind, Captain?"

"How quickly do you think you could synthesize a pheromone from their bodies?"

"Ah, I think I see where your head's at. You want to cover the rovers with their pheromone, which will prevent the hornets from believing they're a threat, is that right?"

"That's exactly right. How soon?"

"Eh, I can get one made pretty fast, but we're still taking a chance. The sun's out. They usually come out during the day. I might not have enough time."

"Let's do it," Thomas said. "Howard, get your rovers ready. They're going in."

***

"On it." Howard Tate turned to face Charity. The red-headed biologist shrugged and began collecting her gear.

"Going right back where I just came from. I guess I should've had this stuff in the Growler to begin with."

She glanced in General Kilmore's direction. He was chomping on a cigar and rolling his eyes, with his phone pressed against his ear. On the other end of the line was probably some politician, either trying to give useless pointers on how to handle the situation, or demanding minute-by-minute updates. Either way, the expression on his face suggested he was fantasizing about throwing the moron into the hornets' nest.

"…No, we have not started yet… Because we're taking another precaution before we begin… Yes, we are ready to use missiles on the nest, but we'd like to keep that as our Plan B strategy... Why? Because new findings suggest the queen is deep underground. She'll be hard to kill, even if we lay into the mountainside with everything we have..." Kilmore shook his head, enduring another monologue from the idiot on the line. Finally, he partially cupped his mouth. "Oh, damn. Senator, I think I'm losing the signal. These hills tend... interfere... signal..." He ended the call and took a much-needed draw on his cigar before looking to Charity. "Son of a bitch couldn't run a hot dog stand if his life depended on it, and here he is trying to tell me how to contain a mutant wasp outbreak."

"Well, sir, when it's time for your next phone call, all you'll have to say is 'Mission accomplished. Now go away.'"

Kilmore smirked. "Even that's too long of a conversation." He took another draw on the cigar and looked in the direction of the nest. "It used to be sarcasm when I'd say I'd rather be fighting monsters than dealing with politicians. But here I am..." With that in mind, he switched his phone off.

"Speaking of fighting monsters..." Charity lifted a briefcase and loaded it into the Growler. Archer approached and helped her load the rest of her equipment into the back of the vehicle. While she dealt with syringes, portable X-ray machines, and a chemical mixing device, Howard Tate began pushing one of his rather hefty rovers toward the vehicle.

The rover was roughly half of his height and bottom heavy. It stood on a base with treads on its left and right sides like an Abrams tank. Four arms protruded from its main body, each one equipped with multiple tools, most of which were intended for sample collecting. Today, they holstered multiple bottles of Howard's newly synthesized pesticide.

He knelt at the base to hoist it into the Growler, grunting from the manual labor. He shot a glare at Archer as he assisted Charity with the comparatively small equipment. Once the sniper was finished, he grabbed his rifle and climbed into the passenger seat.

"Oh, thanks!" Howard shook his head and gripped the rover. "Ya suck, ya know that, Archer?"

"What's the matter, Howard?" Charity said with a chuckle. "That bot too much for you?" As she spoke, she took the other side of the rover and heaved it into the Growler.

Howard brushed his hands together. "For your information, that 'bot' is a Model K34 Ground Level Reconnaissance Drone. It has been very useful in identifying meteor particles in the soil, which in turn, helps us identify risk areas for mutations."

Charity chuckled a second time. It never failed to amuse her how Howard spoke about his machines as though they were his own children. She tapped him on the shoulder and climbed into the driver's seat.

"Hurry up and get in. Unless you'd like me piloting your K14-blah-blah-blah drone."

"K-*34*! Ground Level Reconnaissance Drone. You'd think someone with two PhDs could remember that. And to your point... hell no!" He boarded the vehicle and buckled in, jolting in his seat as Charity floored the accelerator. She whipped the vehicle around the natural obstacles provided by the forest, causing Howard to sway back and forth. "You know, I'm very close to making a remark about women drivers!"

Charity veered to the left. "Good, because you drive like an old lady."

Before long, the command post was out of sight. The trio were surrounded by trees, which partially obscured the enormous mound to the northeast.

A shot of Archer's sniper rifle made Howard jump in his seat. The sniper lowered the barrel and watched his target plummet from the canopy.

"Stop here."

Charity was already hitting the brakes. "Perfect. Cuts our trip in half." She put the vehicle in park and stepped out. Archer was watching the trees with caution. The fact that one hornet was patrolling the sky was an indicator their hunting routine was about to begin.

He stood guard while the two scientists moved their equipment to the fresh corpse. Fortunately, Archer had shot it through the head, leaving the abdomen intact.

Charity moved her x-ray scanner over the bug and waited for the images to appear on her tablet.

"Ah-ha! Perfect. Target acquired."

She took a small drill and pressed the bit to the underside of the hornet's abdomen. Yellow fluid oozed from the wound as she bored a hole through the armor, forming a path for her syringe needle.

That went in next.

"How's it coming?" Thomas asked over the radio.

"Working on it," Howard replied.

"Okay. But how long? We're starting to see more activity."

"Captain, we understand the situation at hand," Howard said. "Just let us do our jobs."

BANG!

Howard's eyes went to the sky, then gradually to the ground as another hornet drone succumbed to Archer's marksmanship. As the echo faded away, a new sound took its place.

Buzzing wings.

Howard's throat tightened. "So, um, Charity? How long?"

"Shut up, Howard!" she replied, grimacing while extracting the pheromone from the insect's abdomen.

BANG!

Another hornet fell, landing just a few meters from the group.

Howard rushed to the Growler and pulled an M4 carbine from the back passenger seat. He returned to his rover and kept watch. The droning of wings was intensifying, as was the exchange of radio chatter.

The first to speak was Renee. *"Falcon here. We've got a few bugs coming out of the main entrance."*

"How many?" Kilmore asked.

"Maybe half a dozen. Got a few more coming out through the center mound. Soon we'll have the whole circus."

The next voice was Lieutenant Balenger's. *"Guard One here. We just bagged a couple hornets attempting to exit through the tunnels. Safe to say, they know something's up."*

Charity, already anticipating a repeat of the 'how much longer?' question, snatched her radio.

"I've extracted the sample. Give me a few minutes, I'll have a duplicate synthesized." As she spoke, she extracted the needle and fed it into the chemical mixing machine. A computer analyzed all of the specific aromatic compounds and acids. A geometric series of numbers flashed on the screen, gradually forming a long mathematical formula for replication. "Okay, got it! I need another minute to put the ingredients together."

Archer let off a series of gunshots. Charity instinctively reached for her sidearm, sensing the approach of bloodthirsty insects. She looked to the north, seeing the segmented shape of one of them bearing down on her. Its body was vertical, the abdomen twitching, stinger protruding.

The sniper reloaded his rifle and immediately put a round through its head. As the bug plummeted, two more took its place. They identified their human targets and moved in.

Howard unleashed a few bursts from his carbine. One of the hornets was struck through the abdomen. Drizzling yellow blood, it zipped to its right, circling the group while its companion went in the opposite direction. Howard tried to follow the first target with the muzzle of his rifle. He fired off a few rounds, only to curse under his breath after missing. The damn thing was too fast, even for the most proficient of marksmen...

BANG!

...except for Archer.

After putting a sniper round through Howard's target, he pivoted and set his sights on the other. The motion of his rifle muzzle followed the hornet's exact movements, seemingly guided by some kind of spiritual force.

With a squeeze of the trigger, Archer exploded the hornet's thorax. The head and abdomen broke away, as did the legs and wings.

Howard gazed at the drone he had shot through the abdomen. Shrugging, he looked at Archer.

"I slowed that one down for you."

Archer sported a brief cheery grin before turning his weapon toward the sound of rustling tree branches. Howard stood beside him, carbine pointed at the small gathering of insects.

"Damn it. We took too long."

"Not too late," Archer said. He went to the Growler and switched his sniper rifle out for an AA-12 automatic shotgun. He loaded a fresh drum and stood between the hornets and his teammates. "Finish up your science project. I'll mingle with our guests."

Howard backed toward Charity. He had no doubt Archer had them covered. In addition to his AA-12, he had two Desert Eagles, loaded with .50 caliber rounds holstered to his thighs. Generally, Howard would consider dual-welding those monster handguns as the most impractical thing imaginable. Except, this was Archer, the guy who could shoot the nuts off a fruit fly from a hundred yards out with a sniper rifle, fired from the hip.

The two scientists were in good hands. As long as they didn't take much longer.

"How's it coming?" he said to Charity.

She groaned. "You asking will not speed things up." She barely finished speaking when the sound of machine-gun fire thundered in the sky above them.

"We've got hornets taking to the skies," Thomas said. He proceeded to give instructions to the helicopter squadron before he and Renee joined the fray.

Charity cleared her throat. "Just another minute."

Repeated booms from Archer's automatic shotgun made the scientists shudder.

"Gonna be a long-ass minute," Howard replied.

***

"Hope you don't get airsick, Captain!" Renee said. No sooner did the words exit her lips did she bank to starboard and fire the forward machine guns.

Behind the droning of the rotors, Thomas could hear the shredding of exoskeleton and the raining of body parts onto the hillside. He gripped the door gun and joined the party. Several bugs were scurrying out of the main entrance. They spread their wings, ready to join the dozen or so brethren already in flight.

Thomas aimed the machine-gun down at them and unleashed its fury. Two of the hornets were cut down before they could take to the sky. Snipers, positioned all around the area, began popping off rounds, cutting down the flow of insects as they exited the nest.

Renee rotated the *Falcon* twenty degrees to port and gunned down another pair of hornets. The other choppers in the area began evasive maneuvers. Despite the casualties G.O.R.E. Sector had inflicted, there were still an increasing number of hornets taking to the sky. Not only did the queen reproduce at an alarming rate, but her brood matured equally as fast.

It was enough for Thomas to wonder if this species skipped the larva stage completely and emerged from their eggs as fully-formed hornets. At the moment, there were at least two dozen of them in flight.

"Eagle Six, you've got two coming up on your six."

"Copy that! Evasive maneuvers. Gunner can't shake them off. They're big, but still hard to hit."

"Eagle Three to Falcon. We've got one near our tail rotors. Everywhere we go, he tries to follow. I really don't want him caught up in the blades."

"Hang on," Renee said. She rotated the vessel fifty degrees to port. Eagle Three was a couple hundred feet away from the *Falcon*. The chopper was moving every which way, like a hummingbird inspecting an assortment of flowers. Like the pest it was, the hornet hovered near its tail, looking for a place to sting. Making matters worse was a second bug flying near the cockpit, studying the glass and the men behind it.

"Get us closer, Renee," Thomas said.

"On it." She banked the *Falcon* to port until they were fifty feet away.

Sensing a new target moving in aggressively, the hornet near the tail rotors turned to its right. It spotted Thomas and decided to move in for the kill, only to get split apart by a barrage of bullets.

He swiveled the gun toward the other hornet. It was trying to move in, deterred only by the intense spinning of the rotors. It backed up, providing just enough space for Thomas to safely discharge a burst of gunfire.

The hornet was smacked out of the air, trailing a thin line of yellow blood as it fell.

"Thanks, Captain… Holy crap! You've got some coming up on ya!"

"Yeah, I see them." Renee put the *Falcon* in reverse, keeping distance between it and the three bugs advancing on her twelve o'clock. The forward guns did their work, cutting the trio to pieces with ease. "Ah-ha-ha! Dummies. Seriously thought they could do a bum rush and—"

CRASH!

"Aw, hell."

The bug had come up from directly underneath her. It had latched onto the nose of the *Falcon* and steadily made its way to the cockpit door.

Thomas leaned outside, barely getting a view of the insect as it peered through the portside cockpit window. He drew his .40 caliber sidearm and extended it toward the hornet's twitching abdomen.

The bug spasmed as multiple holes formed in its lower body. Its wings extended and vibrated, lifting it off the cockpit. It did not retreat, but rather repositioned itself for another attack. Unfortunately, it had unknowingly put itself directly downrange of Thomas' machine-gun.

A stream of bullets successfully reduced the insect into an assortment of falling parts.

"You alright, Renee?"

"Never better!"

"Wouldn't have been if that bug had three more seconds."

"Oh, Captain. You worry too much."

"On that note…" Thomas adjusted his mic. "Howard? Charity? How's it going down there?"

***

"Damn it!" Charity ducked, narrowly avoiding the six talons of a very angry hornet. Howard had fallen on his back, having avoided an even narrower close call. The hornet's stinger had grazed his jacket, resulting in a seven-inch rip and a stain from three ounces of venom.

"Holy…" He turned his eyes back to the bug. It was hovering overhead, ready to make a second go at him. Howard struck first, planting six rounds through its thorax. The bug struck the ground beside him, its legs and abdomen twitching. Even as life left its body, it was still programmed to attack.

Howard rose to his feet and put a round through its head.

"Whew!"

Archer's auto-shotgun thundered as he cut down a small horde of bugs assembling nearby. Some fell to the ground and others retreated farther into the forest, only to circle back.

In the moment of reprieve, Howard helped Charity to her feet. She tapped her vest in search of her radio, ultimately locating it.

"Charity? Howard? Archer? Someone respond, damn it!"

"We're here," Charity replied.

"Are you alright?"

"I've completed synthesizing the pheromone. We just need to… oh, crap."

"Oh crap? I don't like 'oh crap'. What's happening?"

Charity and Howard stood in stunned silence, gazing at the damaged rover. It had been knocked onto its side, with one of its wheels damaged. The axle was bent inward and the left rear arm joint had jammed.

"The rover is damaged," she said to Thomas.

"Hang on, I think I can fix it," Howard said.

"You sure?" Thomas asked.

"Yeah, just… oh hell!"

More bugs swooped in from the maze of pine canopy. Archer immediately went on the defense, mutilating one of them as soon as it appeared.

"What's going on?"

"More hornets," Charity replied. She drew her pistol and joined the action. Several holes popped in the head of an attacking hornet, ending its life before it could sting her. "We just need another minute."

As she spoke, she emptied her magazine at another hornet coming at her. It took numerous hits to the abdomen, but being the perfect soldier, it kept coming with no regards to its own safety. Only a headshot from Archer ended its assault.

Charity reloaded her pistol and helped Howard with the rover.

"Keep it upright," he said. "I think I can straighten the axle."

***

For Thomas, time seemed to slow down to a halt. The plan was falling apart in spectacular fashion. His team was literally getting swarmed, and only a fraction of the nest was attacking so far. In a few minutes, there would be hundreds of hornets filling the sky. By then, Charity, Archer, and Howard would have no hope of survival.

"We need to help them."

He heard Renee shift in her seat. "We *are* helping them. Trust them, Captain. They know what they're doing. Besides, Archer is with them. They might as well have a whole battalion protecting them."

Thomas tried to take her words to heart. His focus was shattered by the rattling of distant gunfire and the sight of black shapes zipping throughout the battle zone. Several hornets briefly emerged between some treetops on the west side, nearing his team's location.

No matter how hard he tried, he could not shake the echo of gunfire he heard through their radio transmission. They were in trouble and it did not appear time was on their side.

The gut-wrenching feeling of worry was accompanied by a shadow of guilt. If anything happened to them, he would have a hard time living it down.

It was settled. Thomas had made a decision.

"Renee, move in on their location."

"Okay. That's a good idea. Let's provide air cover for them."

"No, you're picking them up," Thomas said.

"Huh?!"

"You heard me. Don't argue." Thomas leaned into his mic. "Archer, plant a smoke marker. We're heading your way."

A few moments later, a brand-new tornado of red smoke stretched over the forest. Renee, uncharacteristically silent, moved in on the marker, gunning down a few bugs along the way.

She lowered the *Falcon* until it was right above the treetops, giving Thomas a view of his teammates. Charity and Howard were hastily trying to fix the rover whilst Archer continued providing defense. He was essentially a human turret, blasting into the sky, barely breaking a sweat in the process.

Thomas used his machine-gun to help eliminate the hornets in the vicinity. In the process, he looked for any clearing between the trees suitable for the *Falcon* to set down. Fortunately, there was one only sixty yards northwest of their current position.

"Set down there."

"Captain, I think you should…"

"Ensign Larson, I'm not gonna tell you again."

The tone, as well as the use of her last name and rank, drove the point home. The Captain was not going to tolerate any arguing with this one.

She moved into the clearing and set down.

With an M4 carbine in hand, Thomas stepped out and sprinted across the relatively short distance to the rest of Raptor Pack.

Howard and Charity shared the same bewildered expression seeing him emerge from the woods. Archer's confusion was much more subtle. Mainly a brief squint in his eye before returning his focus on watching out for more insects.

"Hi, Captain," Howard said. "I think I can fix it."

"Dr. Tate?" Thomas began, his tone seizing the doctor's attention. "Can those cannisters be activated without the rover?"

"Um, yes," Howard replied. "They can be set off remotely just like an explosive. They each have a triggering mechanism near the nozzle."

"Perfect," Thomas said. "All three of you, get your asses on the *Falcon*."

"What?" Charity perked up. "You want us to evacuate?"

"What about the rover?" Howard asked.

"There's no time," Thomas said.

Charity stood up, her entire face wrinkling. "So, you're just going to blow up the nest?"

Thomas shook his head. "I'm gonna try something else, first. Now, get aboard. Archer, go with them."

The soldier hit him with a wall of eye contact that could be felt in his soul. Though nothing was said, Thomas could feel a heated monologue full of profanities and a few remarks regarding the Captain's lack of faith in the team. Being the disciplined soldier, he kept his words to himself and followed his orders.

"What about you?" Howard asked.

"Don't worry about me. Now move!"

The three team members ran past to the aircraft, leaving Thomas alone with the rover and the Growler. He removed the three cannisters from the rover and placed them in the passenger seat.

He sat at the wheel and pointed the vehicle at the main entrance. A few moments later, Renee's voice came through his headset.

"Team's aboard, sir. Waiting on you."

"Don't. Get in the air. I've got something to do."

"Sir? Captain?"

Thomas deactivated his radio and gunned the engine. He kept one hand on the wheel and the other on the grip of his carbine. The hornets were busy with the helicopters and perimeter units. Only a couple took notice of the vehicle rapidly approaching the center of their hive.

The trees were spaced out far enough for Thomas to weave around without losing too much speed. He could see the elevation where the nest had elevated. The Growler reached the slope, forcing him to floor the accelerator to maintain speed.

The pair of hornets tracking him attempted to move in for the kill. Thomas, who had spotted them in his peripheral vision, extended his carbine in their direction. Unable to properly aim the rifle, he simply let out a wild spray of bullets. To his relief, he managed to hit both of them.

"Maybe I absorbed some of Archer's skill," he joked to himself.

He continued up the slope. There were no more trees. Just clear, empty space with little vegetation. What used to be here had been uprooted in favor of hollowing the earth for the good of the colony.

The top of the hill was a couple dozen yards away. A pair of hornets emerged and gazed down at the intruder.

He returned their greeting with a second spray of bullets, shattering the windshield of his Growler in an effort to neutralize the guards. One of the bugs fell where it stood. The other took a few devastating hits to the mandibles, knocking it backward into the nest.

Thomas wiped away a few glass shards from his lap and face, finding a small line of blood in his fingers. His cheek and brow was cut. Minor injuries compared to what he was risking. Considering what he was attempting, his time on Earth could very well be counting down to its last tick.

Better me than my team.

With a deep breath, he ascended the final few yards, hitting the brakes after spotting the rugged edge of the opening.

Many of the horde broke away from the choppers and perimeter and began moving toward the nest's center. One of the guards had probably let out a chemical signal, alerting the others that a threat had broken through the defenses. The air around him vibrated from the combined wing movement, producing bizarre soundwaves that assaulted his senses.

Grabbing the cannisters, he stepped out of the vehicle and brought them to the edge of the entrance. There, he caught a brief glimpse of the empire down below. It was a typical honeycomb shape, only hundreds of feet wide. The walls were full of white fiber sealing large eggs inside hexagonal cells. And throughout the nest were at least a hundred hornets, many of whom were emerging from the bottom chamber after tending to the queen.

Thomas exhaled sharply and tossed the cannisters in.

"Sorry for gassing up the place." He hopped into his Growler and reversed it down the hill. He switched his radio back on and shouted into his mic. "Detonate the cannisters!"

He reentered the forest, cutting the wheel left, then right to avoid some of the trees. Several hornets were in front of his shattered windshield, keeping pace.

Thomas turned his eyes forward and discharged his rifle at his pursuers.

CRASH!

He grunted, his head whipping back against the top of his seat. A glance over his shoulder confirmed he hit a tree.

The insects closed in, angling their abdomens to plant a series of fatal stings into their enemy. Thomas remained in his seat, eyes unblinking, hand reaching for his sidearm. The job was done. So long as his team was safe, he did not care what happened to himself.

He raised his pistol and pointed it at the nearest hornet.

"Let's go."

Right then, the bugs halted whatever they were doing. Had it not been for the buzzing of their wings, it would have appeared as though they had frozen in place.

All at once, they raced toward the nest.

At the same time, radio chatter filled Thomas' ears. It was Howard Tate, communicating with General Kilmore.

"Affirmative, sir. Gas has been deployed. Looks like it's working."

"I think the queen's letting out a distress signal," Charity added. *"The hornets are picking up on it and racing to her aid."*

"Joke's on them," Kilmore said. *"They're heading straight to their deaths. Anyone have eyes on Captain Rodney?"*

"He's on the hill," Renee said. *"Captain? You alright?"*

"I'm good," Thomas replied.

"Want me to pick you up, or you prefer to make it to basecamp yourself?"

Thomas closed his eyes, leaned his head back, and exhaled slowly through his nostrils. She was pissed. All of them were pissed.

"Great. I'd rather put up with the damned insects," he muttered to himself before replying to Renee. "First thing's first, Raptor Pack. Prep one of Howard's spare rovers. Let's get some more cannisters into the lower chamber and finish off the queen."

CHAPTER 3

Oh, for the love of God. Please get a signal.

Hayden Spencer twisted the radio knob, praying he would get more than broken bits of noise. Alas, that was all the antenna would get him. As for his phone, all he got was the white dotted 'circle of death'. To top it all off, he had forgotten to take his CDs out of Mary's car back at home.

No matter what, he was doomed to endure the sounds of gameplay in the backseat.

What was usually an appeal for vacationing in the hills of Pleasant County, Wyoming, was now a detriment. Generally, he loved having no signal on his radio or phone. It served as a great way to tune out the digital world and focus on what nature intended for mankind to enjoy.

But today? There was nothing he wouldn't give to blast that radio to the max and tune out the sounds of gnarling and blasting behind him. The repetition of annoying sound effects coming from Franklin and Billy's stupid handheld game consoles had put him in a sort of trance. He was conscious, but unable to put together a coherent thought. He had asked his sons to turn the volume down on their devices, only to get an 'okay' response, yet no change in the noise level.

It wasn't just the noise level, but the *type* of noise. Hayden was thirty-eight. His time of video games had ended with the good ol' *GameCube* and original *PlayStation.* And even by then, he had pretty much grown out of it. Nowadays, games had grown too graphic and weird for his tastes, and he found the addicting nature of such things off-putting. Especially the online chat stuff. At least having no internet connection killed any chance of them doing online gaming. That was the worst in Hayden's opinion. It was as though the weirdos they played with seemed more interested in spewing curse words than playing the game.

Coming out here and getting in touch with nature sounded like the best way to connect with his kids at first. Sitting around at home, staring at the belongings of his beloved Mary wasn't doing anybody any good. All it did was make them dwell on her recent passing all the more.

The last six months was a constant nightmare. Hayden had convinced himself it would end with Mary's passing. At least the pain, nausea, and anxiety caused by her cancer would be over. She was a God-loving woman, so he leaned on the comfort that she was in a better place. Though he believed it to be true, it did not awaken him from the nightmare.

Living without his wife of thirteen years, even with the mental prep of the last six months, was endless torture. The boys coped in their own ways, mainly video games, movies, and comic books. Up until now, Hayden did little to change their habits. He figured it was their way of getting through this ordeal. But after three weeks of endless screen time and almost no family interaction, he chose to take action.

Already, he was regretting that decision. Attempts at small talk were fruitless. All he got were one-word answers, with the exception of 'eh, I don't know' to almost every question he asked them.

Emotional frustration and the constant audible bombardment of gameplay got the better of Hayden. He had enough self-control to not lose his temper, but only because he chose an alternative option—one he felt was just as bad. He mentally checked out.

Screw it. Let the kids rot their brains out. Maybe one day they'll outgrow this stuff. He scoffed at the thought. *Won't hold my breath, though.*

The only thing he had going for him today was that the four-hour road trip to his riverside cabin was nearing its end. He focused on the nature surrounding him. Twice now, he spotted a decent-sized elk. He tried pointing them out to Billy and Franklin, who responded with a disinterested 'cool'. They probably did not even look up from their screens.

As they got farther into the county, any view of the horizon was erased by the forest and uneven ground. The familiar landmarks and the memories they sparked activated a small dopamine hit for Hayden. One of them was the fork in the road near David Tee's gas station. Usually, he liked stopping there for a few last-minute refreshments before driving the final ten minutes to the cabin. Today, for some reason, it was closed.

"Odd. Hope everything's alright," he thought aloud.

"Hmm?" It was the first sound Billy made in over twenty minutes. Hayden decided to take advantage of it.

"Oh, the gas station's closed. You know how David is."

"David?"

"Yeah. We call him Mister Tee." Hayden sniggered at the reference, then frowned at the lack of response from his sons. "He's the owner of the station. You remember him."

Billy and his older brother Franklin shrugged.

Hayden groaned. "We see him every time we come up here… Ugh. Anyway, he's always there. I'm just saying, it's a little unusual for the shop to be closed."

"We're not almost out of gas, are we?" Franklin said. It was the one genuine bit of urgency he expressed that was unrelated to the game on his Nintendo Switch.

"No, we still have over a quarter tank. I can come back tomorrow and see if the station is open." Hayden tilted his rearview mirror to get a look at the boys.

What was meant to be an admiring glance immediately turned into a quiet criticism of Franklin's hair. It was shaggy and poorly kept. His shirt wasn't much better. The twelve-year-old was not goth by any means, but he did wear baggy shirts that were a size too big.

Billy was a little better, though mainly because his mother was a little more strict with his appearance. It was a standard she held up to the day she died. She did not get on Franklin's case quite as much, often mentioning to Hayden that he was going through his 'tween stage'.

All he could do was hope she was right.

"Damn it!" Franklin snapped at his game.

"Hey, hey! Watch your mouth," Hayden said.

"Uh-huh."

Hayden sighed, warning himself about starting an argument. The goal of this trip was to find some kind of inner peace, not add more stress.

"What exactly are you playing, anyway?"

"It's called *Planet Defense,*" Franklin said. "You defend the world from an army of alien bugs."

"Oh. Charming," Hayden said.

"I hope they make a new one," Billy said. "Maybe they could make a new version about those G.O.R.E. Squad guys."

"G.O.R.E. Sector. Not squad," Franklin said. "But yes, that sounds dope."

Hayden could not suppress his groan.

"You don't like G.O.R.E. Sector?" Billy asked.

Hayden bit his lip. Which was worse, having no conversation and listening to stupid video games, or discussing current events? At least the latter could be educational.

"No. I don't."

"Why?" Billy asked. "They saved the world from those big wasps."

"And tried keeping it a secret," Hayden said. "No, son. They're not heroes. Frankly, I don't know what makes them so special. There's nothing they do that the National Guard can't. If you ask me, it's just another excuse for the government to expand itself."

"Whatever you say, Dad," Franklin said.

For once, Hayden believed his game-addicted kid was the smarter one in this conversation. He chastised himself for getting into a debate with a ten and twelve-year old about the politics of a new military organization. Hayden didn't trust anything that involved secrets. That was just his nature. The way he figured it, if someone wanted to keep something out of the public eye, it usually meant they had something to gain. Probably something illegal. For all he knew, the fear of mutations would be used against the public to pave the way for more government overreach.

Nope, he did not see those G.O.R.E. Sector guys as heroes. At most, they were probably pawns in a chess game of politics. He chose not to continue the topic.

Luckily, the perfect distraction was just a few minutes away.

He drove along a couple miles of winding road, with no street signs or traffic lights to hinder his progress. At the end of this stretch of pavement came a large hillside, granting him a nice view of the south side of Tusk Mountain. The south end of that large lump of earth was made mostly of jagged rock, making it an ideal spot for mountain climbers. More importantly, it signified the end of the long journey… and freedom from listening to those game consoles.

He took a right turn into a long dirt road, piercing a mile into the woods. The long driveway angled northeast, concluding at the large gravel parking space alongside his two-story cabin.

There it stood, looking just the same as the day he last left it.

"Here we are."

The kids put their games down, seemingly out of necessity than choice. As soon as the truck parked, they stepped out and started heading for the front door.

"Hey, hey!" Hayden said. He pointed at the bed of the truck. "Help me unload the truck before you make yourselves at home. If you think I'm doing this by myself, you've got another thing coming."

Both kids sighed, and swaggered toward the truck.

While they grabbed their bags, Hayden took a moment to take in the sights. Up to the northwest was the rocky side of Tusk Mountain, partially obscured by forest. The front yard needed to be trimmed.

He turned his eyes to the right, finding the entrance to a trail on the northernmost side of the yard. Forty yards in that direction was the only other property in this part of the woods, Jack Tracy's cabin. Maybe later, Hayden would walk that way and offer a hello if the guy was in. Judging by the tire treads he saw on the jeep trail on the way in, he probably was.

The cabin itself was a welcome sight. Constructed out of home-grown cedar wood, it was his home away from home. This year was the first in which he and Mary did not make any winter or spring trips, for obvious reasons. As welcoming as the sight was, it also brought about a hint of sadness. If Hayden had known his most recent trip with Mary would have been the last, he would have done more to make the most of it.

He shook his head, severing the train of thought from his mind. Instead, he fixated on the dock. The river moved steadily in a southeastern direction, grazing against the wooden dock and his twelve-foot aluminum boat. It was over a hundred feet wide at this section with a depth of twelve feet at the middle. When he wasn't reading or hiking, Hayden spent much of his time fishing for trout. His rods were stored in a shed located behind the cabin.

In fact, fishing would be the first thing he would do. Second, technically. First, he needed to unpack.

CHAPTER 4

"Oh boy! Got a straggler!"

Lieutenant Wayne Belanger took aim with his M27 Infantry Rifle. Captain Rodney's strategy of having men guarding each tunnel entrance proved to be wise. Once the chemical payload was dispersed inside of the hive, the entire colony went haywire. Almost all of the bugs raced to the aid of their queen and unborn siblings, unaware they were diving straight to their own deaths.

The result was a storm of subterranean vibration. Each hornet was doomed the moment they reentered their nest. Through their sides, they breathed in the lethal chemical mixture, which immediately began shutting down their respiratory and circulatory systems.

Most died in service of the colony, trying and failing to rescue their queen and her eggs. In a strange, and almost humorous twist, a few of them seemingly made a run. Those who exited through the main entrance atop the cone-shaped structure were cut down by helicopters and snipers.

Others, like the one in Belanger's sights, attempted an escape through the tunnels.

The bug poked its head out of the ground, its large antennae twitching upon detecting the nearby threat. It turned its head and spotted the human pointing the loud weapon at its face.

Then its head exploded.

Belanger lowered his muzzle and whistled a cheer for himself. "Sorry. Should've quit while you were a*head*." He glanced at the three men guarding the entrance with him, half-expecting a chuckle or some other acknowledgement of his one-liner. What he got were a few shrugs, some shaking heads, and a snort. "What?"

The soldiers cleared their throats and acted as though nothing was wrong.

"Huh? Oh, um, nothing, sir," Kove said. He avoided eye contact with the Lieutenant.

"What is it?" Belanger said. The smirk on his face put the soldier at ease enough so he could speak freely.

"The one-liners, sir. They're… how can I say this eloquently…"

After a moment of awkward silence, one of the other soldiers stepped forward. His nickname was Stewie, and he was known for having a way with words.

"You know when a dog barfs, then tries to eat it, then barfs again?"

Belanger stood there, jaw slightly agape for several moments before responding. "You think my one-liners are best described as *that*?!"

Stewie shrugged. "I mean, maybe once in a while they're good enough for me to leave out the second barf, but otherwise—"

"Alright, you bunch of jackasses. I see how it is." Belanger turned southwards, putting his back to his men while making a radio call to his superiors. "Guard One to Raptor Pack. Can you provide any update?"

"In a hurry to leave?" Thomas asked.

"Somewhat. I'm stuck out here with three bozos."

The third soldier, Lent, hit the Lieutenant with a sour glance. "What'd I do?! I was just standing here."

"Ah, I saw the stupid grin on your face when Stewie made his barf comment," Belanger replied.

"We've deployed a second drone into the queen's chamber. We're literally ten seconds away from putting a stop to all of this."

"Good to hear, sir," Belanger said. He sniggered. "Giving the queen a whiff of some bad gas, I see. Should lay off the Taco Bell."

He glanced at Kove, Stewie, and Lent. Just like before, they shut their eyes and shook their heads.

Kove rubbed a hand over his forehead, muttering under his breath, "World's most elite military unit, ladies and gentlemen."

As it turned out, their thoughts were communal with the Captain's.

"Eh, nice one, Lieutenant. That was, eh… Oh, look at that, the drone is in the chamber. Gotta go."

Belanger bit his lip, enduring teasing chuckles from his teammates.

"So, Stewie," Kove said. "Since the Lieutenant did not say we could stop speaking freely, would you care to describe that one for us?"

Stewie relished the opportunity. "With pleasure." He looked to Lent, expecting a word of encouragement of ridiculing Belanger. Instead, the infantryman had a tense look on his face. He was studying the ground, weapon gripped tightly. "What's the problem?"

"I don't know," Lent said. "Thought I felt something. A tremor. Almost as though something was moving under the ground."

The rest of the squad stood silent. Belanger put his hand to the grass, feeling a hint of a tremor coming from the south. He peeked into the hornet tunnel, then shook his head.

"It's nothing. They've commenced the attack on the queen. She's in the middle of her death throes."

Lent kept his eye on the grass, unconvinced by the Lieutenant's explanation, but unable to provide one of his own.

"Yeah, I guess so."

Belanger looked south again. He was unable to see the nest behind the block of forest he stood in, but nonetheless, he took glee in imagining the queen's downfall. With her death, the threat of rapidly expanding insect colonies was over. Having partaken in the battle against the first hornet nest, and then defended the town of Telegraph in Ramsey County during the wasp conflict, he knew all too well the danger these insects posed.

Despite a few mishaps during this morning's operation, G.O.R.E. Sector pulled off a victory without sustaining a single casualty. That alone made today a good day.

"So, Stewie? How would you score the Lieutenant's gas line?"

"Well, you know how Madonna got all that plastic surgery, thinking she was making herself look younger…"

The three soldiers started laughing.

Belanger squeezed his eyes shut and sighed. It was *mostly* a good day.

***

Howard Tate sat at his desk in the middle of the command post, hunching forward after feeling crushed by the weight of Raptor Pack and General Kilmore watching over his shoulder.

"Is it working?" the General asked.

"Yes sir," Howard said. "I have a visual. There's the queen right there." He wedged himself back from the computer to allow the others a clear view.

Thomas grimaced, seeing the horrid form of the bloated hornet queen thrashing about in the big underground chamber. Even in the greenish glow of night vision, her disgusting form was enough to churn the stomach. Her wings were still attached, though it was hard to imagine they would have the strength to carry her immense bulk.

She flipped on her back and clawed at the strange cloud that filled her chamber. The few warrior hornets sharing the chamber quickly dropped from the walls and ceiling, having succumbed to the pesticide after a few seconds. The nurse hornets tending to the queen did not last much longer.

Her majesty herself took a minute longer to expire. Maybe she was equipped with a better immune system or simply had a greater will to live. Ultimately, neither proved effective.

After a long exhale, Howard turned in his chair to face the others. "That's it. The queen is dead."

The men and women on the hilltop applauded. The hornet colony was defeated. G.O.R.E. Sector was victorious once again.

"Well done, everybody," General Kilmore said. "Let's wait for the gas to clear out, then we'll begin the cleaning up stage. You know the deal; I want all specimens collected and I want a thorough sweep of the hive. Don't want to leave any stone unturned. Move out, everybody."

A collective reply of "yes sir" filled the air. The men and women of G.O.R.E. Sector divided into their various units and went to work, with Raptor Pack remaining on the hilltop.

He remained by the desk for a few additional moments, eyes locked to the screen, making sure there was not an ounce of life remaining. The morning had too many close calls for his liking. As he figured, it was a miracle they did not suffer any casualties.

"Relax, Captain," General Kilmore said. "It's over."

"You know how it is, sir. It's never over," Thomas replied. A lightbulb switched on in his head as he spoke those words. "As a matter of fact, there's more work we need to do." He switched on his radio. "Raptor Pack to Scout Team Four. Any update?" No response came through. "Scout Team Four, this is Captain Rodney. Acknowledge." Still nothing. Thomas turned around and saw Renee standing with Howard and Charity a few yards behind them. "Hey, Renee? Can you use the *Falcon's* radio to get in touch with Scout Team Four? I can't seem to reach them. Maybe my signal's too weak."

Renee made a half-hearted smirk and spun on her heel. "Absolutely, Captain. You can trust me." She strutted to where she had landed the aircraft, her body language displaying the same aura of discontent as her tone.

Thomas clenched his jaw and looked to the sky, begging Heaven for an easy solution for this drama. The resentment swelling from his teammates could be sensed by the blindest of people. Aside from initially making sure he was okay after he returned from where his Growler had crashed, they hardly made any acknowledgement of his existence. The usual witty exchange had come to a halt. Eye contact ceased except in brief moments where it could not be avoided. All of these were the marks of people who momentarily despised him.

The members of Raptor Pack maintained discipline. None voiced a complaint or an insult. No matter how they felt, they were a military unit at the end of the day.

A part of Thomas wanted to exploit that fact and let the matter die out on its own. After all, his actions were intended to keep them alive. As far as he was concerned, he succeeded.

Despite his best efforts, his internal attempt to justify his decision to himself did not erase his awareness of their resentment. That left only one solution. He had to address it. Technically, he didn't have to. He was the leader of the unit, and if he wanted to, he could tell them to knock it off and follow his lead. But that was not the trait of a good leader, something Thomas had learned from many years of experience. During his Army years, he served under people who only treated their soldiers as nothing more than chess pawns, and those who valued the lives of the personnel they commanded. The latter always made for the better leaders. When issues arose, those commanders addressed them like men, as opposed to dismissing them.

Thomas swallowed. "Damn it." Sometimes, he hated his own code of ethics. Normally, he would hold this off for later in the day and give their tempers a chance to cool. But there was more work to be done. Scout Team Four had discovered a tunnel a few miles west of the hive, meaning Raptor Pack would be spending the rest of the day investigating the area. Thomas would prefer this tension be put to rest before then.

Hoping to rip the band-aid off quickly, he approached Charity, Howard, and Archer. The sniper nodded in his direction, letting the others know the Captain was coming their way.

"Everyone doing alright?" Thomas asked.

"Just dandy, Captain," Howard replied.

Thomas snorted. The deliberate use of his rank was another indicator of how they really felt.

Charity had her hands on her hips. Thomas could tell every fiber of her being wanted to tell him how she really felt.

"Listen, guys. I made a call. I'm not trying to insult all of you. You're instrumental to our ongoing mission. Things were getting out of hand. We were moments away from the rest of the swarm coming out. I made a judgement call."

"Oh, give me a—" Charity shut her jaw. "Pardon me, sir."

"No, go ahead and speak freely," Thomas said. "Out with it."

Charity was quick to take advantage of that liberty. "You were *lucky.* Very damn lucky. Yes, you succeeded, but the way you did it was borderline suicidal. Yes, we had a little setback, but we were a few seconds from getting Howard's drone operational again. Once it was in the tunnel, we would've had a surefire method of eradicating those hornets. But you didn't trust us to complete the task."

"Those things were all over you, Charity," Thomas said.

"We had Archer," Howard said, pointing his elbow at the sniper. "He was doing a pretty decent job. And once you and Renee showed up to help, the area was clear for the moment. It was the perfect opportunity for us to finish up. Except, you wouldn't let us."

Thomas looked to Archer. As usual, the soldier didn't offer a word, but a subtle half-smirk indicated his agreement with the scientists. The sentiment was clear: *Apparently, you couldn't trust me to protect them.*

"I was just trying to look out for you guys," Thomas replied. "It's not about trust or distrust."

"Well, I appreciate your concern, sir," Howard said. "But we're not stubborn children. Nor are we egomaniacs. If we can't handle a situation, we'll say it outright. Even Archer."

"More to the point, we don't need our Captain getting himself killed in our stead," Charity added. "We've already buried a captain. Newsflash, it's not fun. Unfortunately, it's a risk the job carries on its own. The last thing you need to do is add to the risk by making emotionally-fueled snap judgements." She let that last sentence simmer in Thomas' mind for a moment. "Yeah, I know you were doing it for our safety. And we appreciate the concern. Really, we do. But we're going to be in deadly situations. On the regular. If you can't let us do our jobs out of 'fear we might get ourselves killed', then what's the point in having us at all? Because, in case you haven't realized yet, we're frequently going to be in hairy situations that carry the risk of death. We don't jump headfirst into those situations, but like what happened today, improvisation is sometimes necessary to get the job done."

"Improvisation?" Thomas said, raising one eyebrow. "Like what I did with the Growler?"

"Sure, that may have been necessary if there was no better option," Howard said. "But no, she was referring to the plan of synthesizing the hornet's pheromones like you suggested. It was good on-the-spot thinking, which carried a little bit of risk. But less risk than speeding past a quarter-mile of forest while fending off giant bugs with one hand. Like she said, it was only pure luck that you succeeded. It would have been better if you just helped to keep the colony off our backs while we got the rover back online. Oh, speaking of luck… we are all *damn* lucky the detonators worked on those cannisters. Gravity and technology are not always good bed fellows. Something I would've informed you of, had I known what you were up to."

The four of them stood silent, as though they had run out of words to say. Charity sipped on water, having run her throat dry while speaking her piece. Howard dabbed his brow with a handkerchief, having broken more of a sweat from this awkward conversation than this morning's battle with the hive. Archer remained still as a statue, his opinion expressed through an unblinking glare.

Meanwhile, Thomas failed to find the words to say. He was too busy wrestling with his own justifications, as well as facing the reality that everything said to him was true. Only now, it began to dawn on him that, by trying to save his team, he nearly put the lives of hundreds, if not thousands of people at risk. Had he failed, the full force of the hive would have been unleashed. There would have been no time to prep a second chemical strike.

"Captain?"

The group looked to Renee as she approached from the *Falcon,* collectively relieved to have a segue out of their conversation.

"Any luck?" Thomas asked.

"Negative," she replied. "I do have a link to the marker they set up. It's linked to our tablets."

Thomas didn't like it. This radio silence from the scout team was happening directly after they had discovered a tunnel eerily similar to those surrounding the hive. Only two things made sense. Either the men were having equipment failure, or they encountered something—that 'something' likely being another hornet nest. The only way to know for sure was to get over there and find out.

"Okay. Let's saddle up and figure out what's going on. Howard, load up another drone and some cannisters. There's a chance we'll be exterminating another hive."

***

"Guard Two to Three, how are things over there?" Lieutenant Belanger asked over the radio. More than a simple grunt, his job was to lead support units for Raptor Pack, which meant constant radio communication. In this case, he was checking on the other ground units guarding the tunnel entrances.

"No surprises so far, sir. Quiet over here."

"Just the way I like it," Belanger said. "Four, Five, Six, anything to report?"

"Negative for Four."
"Negative for Five."

"Negative for Six."

"Copy that." He moved his mic from his lips and began pacing around the tunnel. Even an experienced soldier like him hated the boredom of idly waiting, even in situations like this.

He stopped, noticing Lent was taking a knee and feeling the ground.

"Trying to become one with the earth?" he asked.

Lent shook his head, his expression the polar opposite from the Lieutenant's snarky grin. "No. You feel that?"

"Feel what? Wait!" Belanger's grin vanished. There was a vibration under their boots.

Stewie and Kove felt it too. With rifles shouldered, they took position near the tunnel entrance, believing another hornet drone was on its way out. Belanger was not convinced, however. He dropped to one knee and put a hand on the ground. The source of the tremor did not appear to be following the trajectory of the tunnel. Also, whatever was causing it appeared to be larger than a standard warrior hornet.

"Guard One to Raptor Pack. Just for clarification, the queen is dead, correct?"

"Captain Rodney here. I'm looking at the rover footage right now. She's dead as a doornail."

The tremors intensified. A deep rumbling continued north for several yards, its force strengthening as it rose to the surface.

Hearing the sound of splitting earth and rock, Belanger and his men raced into the trees. They crossed a hundred feet of forest before arriving at a stretch of rising landscape. This newly formed hill breached, spewing grass and soil like magma from a volcano.

Through the breach came a large black mass, segmented into three parts. Long, spindly legs stretched for ten feet, their claw tips raking the soil as the hornet princess scampered away from her tunnel. Long wings extended and became a blur of motion.

"We've got a runner!" Kove said.

Belanger lifted his rifle with intent to blast the fifteen-foot-long bug before she could take flight. It would have been successful had it not been for a loyal and very violent escort.

Five hornets emerged behind her. Four of them were warrior drones, tasked with defending the princess with their lives. The fifth was slightly larger than them—the prince. His sole job was to go with the princess on a wedding flight.

Off they went, disappearing into the trees with two of the warriors serving as an escort. The other three engaged the human threat on the ground.

Belanger backed away, sweeping his rifle muzzle back and forth to keep up with his target. One of the bugs had its sights on him, hovering back and forth in search of an opportunity to sting. He tapped the trigger, his aim a little wide. The second shot was on point. The hornet dropped from the sky, thorax deflated after being run through.

He ended its deathly thrashing with a shot to the head, then looked to his men. Kove, Stewie, and Lent stood over the corpses of the other two hornets. It was not a victory, however. The bugs were dead, but their mission was successful. They protected their new queen with their lives. Now, she was out to forge a new colony.

"Guard One to Raptor Pack."

"Go ahead," Thomas replied.

"It's not over yet. We've got a new target. A young hornet queen has tunneled out of the nest and is now flying north."

"Any chopper units have visual?"

"Eagle One here. Negative, Captain. She must be moving within the trees."

***

"Damn it! These freaking bugs, I swear it never ends." Thomas turned to look at General Kilmore. "Obviously, we need to go after it, but we need someone to check on Scout Team Four."

"How did our chemical attack not affect her?" Kilmore asked.

"She must've already been in the process of tunneling when we drove Howard's rover into the chamber," Charity said. "She's a princess. She's likely with a prince for a mating flight. Afterwards, she'll find a place to start a new colony."

"Should we worry about the prince?" Thomas asked.

"He'll die soon after the flight, but he'll use whatever life he has left to defend the new queen," Charity said. She switched her radio on and hit the transmitter. "Guard One, did the princess have any escorts?"

"There's a couple warriors and her date," Belanger responded.

"Copy."

"He said they were going north," Howard said. "They already have a head start, but it gets worse. We don't have a tracker on them. They could turn east or west and we won't have any idea."

"Then we better take to the sky and find them," Renee said. She spoke directly to the General, only paying Thomas an obligatory glance. "The forest isn't that dense. Eagle Squadron and I should be able to locate them if we start pursuit now. This is what I do best, sir. I fly fast and I kill things. Let me loose, and I'll have them dead before lunchtime."

General Kilmore nodded. "Go get 'em, Ensign." Renee saluted and raced to the *Falcon*. Archer stepped forward, expressing a willingness to accompany her as a door-gunner. "Best you go with the Captain. I want you guys to head west and figure out what's going on over there. I'll order Lieutenant Belanger to have his men on standby, in case you need quick assistance."

"Yes sir," Charity said. She and Howard quickly began loading supplies into an M1161 Growler. Thomas, meanwhile, watched as the *Falcon* ascended into the sky and flew north.

"Everything okay with your team, Captain?" Kilmore asked.

"Hmm? Oh, yeah."

Kilmore sniggered at his poor attempt at modesty. "I get it. You want to keep them safe. It's all about judgement, Captain. It's knowing when to let your people take risks. I'm not going to reprimand or praise you for today's actions. At the end of the day, the hive was successfully exterminated—save for the lucky princess. It's good you care about them. It's great, actually. I'd rather they be under the command of someone who cares for their well-being than someone who doesn't give a crap. But just know, that caring can be a detriment if you let it."

Thomas absorbed the words and nodded.

"Yes, sir."

Charity hopped in the driver's seat of the Growler and honked. "You coming, Captain?"

"I don't know. You gonna drive?"

"You can trust me enough to do that much," she said.

Thomas hopped into the front passenger seat. "I don't know. I've seen the way you drive. Giant mutated insects are less of a hazard."

"Oh, is that so!"

She gunned the engine, nearly proving Thomas' point. At least the banter was back in full swing.

CHAPTER 5

Hayden Spencer reared his fishing rod back, hoisting the thirteen-inch trout out of the river. It was a little small to keep. Then again, he probably would have thrown it back anyway. He enjoyed fishing for the dinner table, but today, he couldn't seem to find the right mood. The reason was obvious. Mary used to do the cooking.

Meal prep was one of her favorite parts of the day. While many other friends, both male and female, complained about the day-to-day maintenance of family life, Mary embraced it. And damn, she could cook like a pro too. Rarely did that woman whip something up that he did not scarf down. Even the kids rarely complained about what was being served.

The influx of memories brought simultaneous joy and sadness to Hayden. It was the cliché regarding how you do not realize what you had until you lose it. While Hayden never took the quality of his marriage for granted, he certainly did not expect the longevity of their time together to be so short. When one hears the words Until Death Do You Part, it's natural to assume that meant old age.

With his mood to fish evaporated, Hayden tossed the trout back and returned his gear to the shed. He went around to the front of his cabin and went inside.

To his right was the kitchen area, with groceries still bagged and sitting on the countertop. To his left was the living room, with a large sofa and lazy boy chair on opposite sides. Billy was on the chair and Franklin was on the couch. Charging cables connected their game consoles to nearby power outlets, providing new life to their digital asylum.

"Eh-hem!"

Both kids looked to their father, who then pointed a thumb at the groceries they were instructed to unpack.

"Oh, yeah. Sorry," Franklin said. His eyes went back to the screen.

Hayden took a long, slow breath. In that moment, he reminded himself of the guilt he felt after past instances where he lost his cool with his sons. With that in mind, he chose not to snap at them. They definitely deserved it, but some fights were just not worth it. Besides, it would open the floodgates to a whole other river of pent-up feelings.

He hated their lack of interest in anything other than gaming. As a parent who wanted to see them live prosperous futures, it was crushing to know they had absolutely no motivation. Hayden did not necessarily find video games a bad thing, but in this case, they had completely consumed his kids' attention. Every time he tried to introduce them to something new, whether it was an activity or skill, it was impossible to keep their attention. It was always clear their minds were elsewhere.

Sure, they were still young, but it was hard not to compare them to other kids their age. Other kids in their neighborhood were in all sorts of activities, including sports, plays, and even jobs with local markets. Some did some volunteer work, others helped their fathers do construction projects.

And here Franklin and Billy were, seemingly incapable of unbagging groceries.

"Get it done, please," he said.

He gave thought to going to his bedroom upstairs, only to decide that lying in bed dwelling on how crappy life was did not seem like a great idea. Same with sitting on the porch.

Still feeling stiff from the road trip, he decided to walk one of the trails. The exercise would do him good. Maybe the increased blood flow would lift his mood.

Safety came first. He went to the back room and dug his .40 caliber Ruger pistol and his holster from its shelf. Hayden did not consider himself a crack shot, but in most cases he did not need to be. The noise alone was usually enough to deter aggressive animals.

After strapping the holster to his waist, he grabbed a can of Frontiersman bear spray. Over the years, he had only seen a couple of grizzlies. All the same, it was better to be prepared while walking the forest.

He went to the front door, pausing to remind his kids about the groceries. With a groan, Franklin paused his game and stood up to complete his chore. Billy was soon to follow. At least he was less obnoxious about it.

Again, Hayden chose not to make a big issue of it. He stepped outside and turned left to walk the west trail. The sight of bright green vegetation and forest animals lifted his spirits. There was something about being in the forest that was therapeutic to him.

It wasn't long before he spotted a coyote to the north. It glanced in his direction and studied the human, ensuring he was not a threat. In its jaws was a dead squirrel. After determining Hayden was not out to steal its lunch, it proceeded to disappear into the forest.

After walking a hundred yards, he heard some rustling somewhere to his left. He turned to look, catching a glimpse of a pair of deer trotting between some trees. The way they moved conveyed a sense of urgency. Hayden wasn't worried about it. He assumed they had seen the coyote or maybe some wolves. Rarely did either species attack humans around here, so he had nothing to worry about.

Then he saw the scat.

"Oh, shit."

It was a figure of speech and literally what he was looking at. The pile of black feces showed signs of partially digested leaves and berries. It was fresh, meaning whatever bear dropped them was still here. There was no way to tell whether it was a grizzly or a black bear. He hoped for the latter, which typically presented fewer problems.

Some gravelly bellowing sounds up ahead indicated otherwise. Holding his can of Frontiersman in front of him, Hayden inched farther up the trail. The sight of motion a few dozen yards ahead brought him to a halt.

Immediately, he began backing away.

"Great. Just great," he muttered.

There was not one, but *two* grizzlies. They were standing on their hind feet, revealing their nine-foot heights. Both were looking in Hayden's general direction. Their powerful sense of smell had probably detected a whiff of the Chex Mix crumbs that embedded themselves in his shirt during the drive. He could see the bears drop to all fours. Though it was hard to see through the undergrowth, he could tell they were coming his way. They did not appear to be aggressive, but that could change in a heartbeat.

Hayden decided not to take any chances. He let loose a heavy stream of the repellent. Through the white fog were the agitated sounds of two bears turning away. Their curiosity did not outmatch their tolerance of the vile odor.

The sound of rustling undergrowth grew faint as the bears proceeded farther west. Confident they no longer posed a threat, Hayden lowered the cannister and made his way back to the cabin.

So much for walking this trail. Unfortunately, it would be unwise to continue. Maybe tomorrow, the bears would be a safe distance from the trail. The only way to find out was for him to take another hike. For now, it was probably best to stay near the cabin.

When he stepped through the front door, he found Billy and Franklin in the same spots, only this time they had sodas at their side. The groceries had been put away, save for a couple of open chocolate bars which had been left out on the table. Probably a bear's favorite man-made snack.

"Just a head's up, guys. There's a couple of grizzlies out there, so don't wander off, alright?" He suppressed a chuckle. *Like there's any hope of them even leaving the living room.*

"Oh yeah?" Billy said. "Big ones?"

"Yep. I saw them over that way." Hayden pointed out the window to the west trail. He filled the coffee maker with water and loaded up some coffee grounds.

Franklin sat upright on the couch, watching him.

"Gonna offer them up a cup of Joe?"

That got a laugh from his dad.

"Good one. But no. They generally don't like the smell of coffee. It's just a deterrent to keep them from coming up to our cabin. Like I said, it should be fine. It's just a precaution. Plus, you know how I am with coffee."

"What about Mr. Tracy?" Franklin asked. "Does he know about the bears?"

"Hmm." Hayden looked at the north trail. "Yeah, you know? You've got a point. I'll go say something to him. Either of you wanna come?"

"Mm… nah," Billy said. "Maybe tomorrow."

It was back to the gaming for him and Franklin, the latter of whom probably did not even hear his dad's question.

So much for that.

Hayden was out the door again. With the grizzly encounter fresh in his mind, he quickened his pace. He kept a sharp eye on the surrounding forest, this time not out of admiration for nature, but self-preservation.

He could hear a boat motor to the northwest. Only one to have a boat out here, other than himself, would be Jack Tracy. Afraid he would miss his neighbor, Hayden sped up to a jog.

The trail led him to a two-story cabin. It was a little smaller than Hayden's but provided more than enough space for Jack. The guy was very friendly, but was a borderline recluse. To Hayden's knowledge, he had no friends or family. The only company he desired was his own. And maybe the occasional female companion.

Jack was kneeling at his dock with a toolbox at his side. As it turned out, he was doing some maintenance on his boat motor. He had two fishing boats moored to opposite sides of a long, sturdy dock. The one on the left was a sixteen-foot motorboat. It was essentially a glorified aluminum boat with a better outboard and a little more foot space. To the right of the dock was a twenty-four-foot Summerset Premium Bimini pontoon boat.

"Hi! Excuse me, Jack?" Hayden said, waving a hand.

Jack looked at him and waved back. He was a little older than Hayden and far more muscular. A life of chopping wood like a lumberjack and depending on the land proved sufficient on maintaining peak physical condition.

"Hayden! Long time, no see." He stood up and brushed his hands against his jeans. "How've you been?"

"Oh, busy enough, I suppose."

Jack came over and shook his hand. "Better than doing nothing, I suppose. Unless I'm mistaken, it's been a while since you've been out this way. At least, I haven't seen your truck."

Hayden laughed. "You must be out here all the time to know that."

"I am. I ran into some good fortune, which enabled me to retire early," Jack said. "I guess I've become something of a mountain man."

"Good for you," Hayden said.

"Thank you. Oh, hey! How's the wife and boys? They up here with you?"

Hayden faked a smile. He couldn't blame Jack for the question, for he was not aware of Mary's passing. As of late, he had gotten enough sympathy. Plus, he was not up for the awkwardness of telling Jack the truth.

"It's just me and the boys today. They're doing well. Except when it comes to doing their chores."

"Ain't that the truth?" Jack said. "Reminds me of why I didn't have any of my own."

"Right… So, anyway, I thought I'd say hi. Also, I wanted to give you a heads up. I went for a walk a few minutes ago and saw a couple of grizzlies. Full grown pair, by the looks of 'em."

Jack groaned. "Oh, that's just marvelous."

"No kidding. Hopefully, they'll go away," Hayden said. "I managed to spray some repellent. Seemed to make them go west. Hopefully they'll keep heading that direction."

"Good thinking," Jack replied. "I guess, in return, I should give you a heads up… though I'm not sure what to make of this."

He gestured for Hayden to follow him. They went a few dozen yards into the woods where they came across an area of flattened undergrowth. Several ferns and bushes had been uprooted or flattened, with some scraping on the base of nearby trees.

Hayden's eyes widened. "Whoa!"

"Yeah. Not sure what came through here, but it was big."

"Some pissed off moose? Or some grizzlies?" Hayden suggested. It seemed unlikely, but it was the only thing that made even a little bit of sense. Nothing else in this forest was big enough to do this kind of damage. And as far as he knew, there was nobody out here with a bulldozer.

"I'm not sure," Jack said. "It looks like it was coming in from the southwest, whatever it was."

"When did you first see it?"

"This morning. Didn't see what caused it, obviously." Jack cracked a smile and playfully tapped Hayden on the shoulder. "It'd suck if it was one of those meteor mutations we've been hearing about. Am I right?"

Hayden let out a small, unenthusiastic laugh. "Yeah, that would suck."

"Nah." Jack shrugged. "I think it's safe to assume there's nothing to worry about." He turned around and walked back to his cabin.

Hayden stayed behind for a few extra moments, eyes glued to the trail of debris.

"Yeah. Probably."

CHAPTER 6

As Raptor Pack crossed the bridge to the west side of the Naagin River, a flood of transmissions coursed through their radio receivers. Thomas watched the skies, curious if the *Falcon* and any of the chopper units had come this direction.

"Eagle Four here. I've got nothing but trees over by the mountainside."

"Don't think it went that way," Renee said. *"I'm about three miles northeast of the hive. I see some damage to the treetops. Looks like something big was passing through here. Heading twenty-five degrees northeast of my location."*

"Eagle One copies. Proceeding to your pos."

"Maintain a spread of one hundred yards. If you see anything out of the ordinary, speak up."

"General Kilmore here. I've got a squadron of fighter jets coming in from Malstrom Air Force Base. Royal Canadian Air Force and National Guard has been alerted."

"Too bad they won't have any of the fun. I'll have her majesty bagged by noon," Renee said.

"I expect nothing less," Kilmore replied.

An elbow from Charity shocked Thomas from his trance-like state. He looked over at her. "What?"

"Relax, Captain," she said. "They've got it under control. It's not your problem to worry about."

"For Renee, this is just another day in the week that ends in Y," Howard added. "She'll be fine."

Thomas switched out of the air units' channel and put his eyes on the forest.

"How far are we from the beacon?"

Charity made a right-hand turn after clearing the bridge exit. "Just another mile."

"Howard? How many surveillance drones did you bring along?" Thomas asked.

"Three," Howard replied. "Equipped with a camera with a range of five hundred yards, infrared tracking, capable of taking samples, both biological and geological. All three are equipped with a mini-turret under their base, armed with nine-millimeter rounds. Thirty round capacity for each. Not enough to fight a war—especially not one against the type of threats we go up against—but still enough to get on the nerves of a monster. That said, if we need to pack a little extra punch, each drone has a single block of C4 for a suicide run."

Thomas sported a grin and turned to look at the engineer. "You'd actually blow up your precious machines, Dr. Tate?"

"Pride does not follow the sentiment," Howard said. The bitterness in his voice made Thomas and Charity laugh. Howard maintained a sour glare, which intensified after he saw a small grin on Archer's face. As usual, his admiration for his mechanical staff provided amusement for his team members. "Laugh all you want. I'm not stupid. I value the safety of my machines, but not over my own life. Or yours, even if you are a bunch of jerks."

"Oh, stop. You'll make me blush," Thomas said. "I can only imagine the anguish you felt when you drove the rover into the queen's chamber and…"

Charity hit the brakes, cutting him off.

"Oh my God." Her hands were ten and two, her eyes frozen at an alarming sight at their two o'clock.

Thomas followed her gaze. Near the riverside was a heap of green-painted metal, now darkened by a recent fire. A thin trail of smoke continued billowing from it and the surrounding landscape. The smell of charred metal and fuel reached their nostrils.

"Do I see what I think I see?" Howard asked.

Thomas nodded. "Yep." They were looking at the remains of Scout Team Four's IFAV. He gripped his carbine tight and searched his surroundings. "So much for the day's work being over."

Charity pulled up to the ravaged vehicle and parked. All four of them exited their Growler and secured the perimeter.

The IFAV was toast, appearing to have bounced like a ping pong ball before its fuel tank had ignited.

Thomas approached the wreckage and checked the seats. "No bodies. No remains. Does not appear they were in the vehicle when it exploded."

"What happened?" Charity said. "It looks like it's been tossed."

"Hornets, maybe?" Thomas asked.

"Only a mature queen would be strong enough to pull that off," Charity said.

Howard took a look at the vehicle's underside. In its center was a large dent, caused by some sort of impact which had ruptured the fuel tank.

"I don't know if tossed is the right word. 'Launched' is more like it. This damage had to have been caused by a direct hit."

"Maybe the hornets knocked the vehicle on its side and then one of them kamikazed into it," Charity suggested.

"Not likely."

All eyes turned to Archer. As they all knew, the guy rarely spoke. And when he did, it meant something.

He stood next to what appeared to be a small mound by the riverside. A fifteen-foot section of earth had been pushed upward, forming a tiny hill. In its center was a gaping hole. Bits of soil and gravel, from several different layers of earth, had peppered the surrounding area, as though spat from this tiny hilltop.

Archer pointed his sniper rifle at some tire marks leading up to the oddity. "Something emerged from *under* them."

Thomas' detective skills kicked in. A few yards from where Archer stood was an assault rifle. The grass was flattened, as though its owner had been knocked to the ground. Or, more precisely, thrown from the IFAV.

Archer saw it too. He walked to the weapon and checked its magazine, then shook his head at his Captain. The soldier did not fire a shot.

Thomas searched the surrounding area, eventually finding the next clue. Two other rifles lay several yards to the west of the first one. He checked both magazines. Unlike the one near the hole, these had been fired repeatedly.

"They made contact with something. They were shooting toward the river. Archer, you see any blood where you're standing?"

"None, sir," Archer replied. "None by the first gun, either."

"Either these men missed every shot, or whatever they were shooting at had bulletproof skin," Thomas said.

"Another hornet princess, perhaps?" Howard asked. "Makes sense, considering the size of the tunnel."

"Except it formed under the IFAV," Thomas said. "They would not have parked directly on top of it. Also, I don't think the princess would tunnel out like this. What do you think, Charity?"

She was standing at the edge of the burrow, studying the formation of its interior. "It's unlikely. She'd be more focused on deepening her hive. Also, the way this tunnel was formed is not characteristic of hornets."

"What do you mean?"

Charity bit her lip, trying to wrap her mind around what she was looking at. "It angles off at only a few feet. It's too large to have been dug by one of the workers. Also, the walls are too smooth and lacking a residue left by the hornets. They would coat the walls with a syrup-like substance that would maintain the shape of their tunnels. This, I don't know—it looks like something a big worm would make."

Thomas did not like the sound of that. Nor did he care for the next thing he saw.

The ground had been marred by a wide, yet concentrated stream of motion. It originated from the burrow, moving to where the first soldier had gone down before attacking the second two. He followed the trail of flattened grass and damaged vegetation to the north.

Whatever this thing was, it had moved elsewhere. Thomas was certain of two things: It was large and extremely dangerous. Something Scout Team Four had unfortunately learned all too well.

Thomas turned to Archer, who was now moving eastwards into the forest. "Find something?"

"Got a trail, Captain," Archer replied. He continued moving deeper into the forest. Thomas gladly allowed him to take point. Archer's tracking skills far surpassed his own.

Charity and Howard were right behind him, weapons in hand. At the moment, they were leaning on the military side of their training as opposed to the scientific.

It was only a few moments before Howard realized the trail was leading them straight to the beacon. After crossing a few hundred feet of forest, they saw a dish-shaped device staked into the ground. Thirty feet beyond it was a large crater. Raw earth surrounded it, with chunks of dirt tossed in all directions.

Thomas knew the deal. This was not solely the result of a subterranean creature breaching the surface. A real explosion occurred here.

The team secured a perimeter before inspecting the crater.

"Just as I suspected. They planted C4 inside the tunnel with laser tripwire," Thomas said.

"That means something either came in or out," Charity said.

Howard turned a full three-hundred-sixty degrees. "I don't see any remains. What the hell did they kill?"

Thomas took a few glances at the surrounding area. Howard made a good point. There was nothing here. No body. No remains. Nothing.

Except a large, narrow trail leading behind some brush to the east.

"Oh, hell," Thomas groaned. He didn't need Archer's tracking skills to know what happened here. Scout Team Four had marked the burrow, continued their inspection, then responded after hearing the explosion. Realizing the thing was nearby—and worse, not dead despite taking four blocks of C4 to the face—they made the decision to retreat to their patrol vehicle.

"They didn't stay here the whole time. Archer, can you find any other tracks?" he asked. Archer studied the ground for a moment in search of a new trail. He moved north of the tunnel entrance, then nodded at his Captain.

"This way."

Thomas exhaled through his nostrils and watched the trail with a silent fury. G.O.R.E. Sector had suffered three casualties today. Unless their killer was found and destroyed, there was bound to be more.

"Raptor Pack to Guard One."

Lieutenant Belanger was quick to respond. *"Yes, Captain. Go ahead."*

"Assemble your men. I'm going to need you over here. There's another player at large. We're currently working to identify what it is."

"Copy that. We'll mount up."

Thomas turned to face Howard. "Get your drones in the air. I want them searching a three-mile perimeter."

"Aye-aye, Captain," Howard said. He turned around and hurried to their vehicle.

Thomas snapped his fingers at Charity and Archer. "Let's return to the vehicle. We'll follow the trail, but I'd rather be on wheels. For all we know, we'll have to hightail it."

Charity nodded. She took one last look into the mouth of the tunnel. "It's the exact same shape as the other one. I don't know what could have done this."

"I don't know either," Thomas said. His eyes locked onto the flattened section of bushes. "But it wasn't hornets."

CHAPTER 7

If anything good came from that bear encounter, it was the excuse it provided Hayden Spencer to make the cabin smell of coffee. He had brewed his third pot in a row, maximizing the aroma. It was as much for his own enjoyment as it was a bear deterrent. Since having kids, he had become a coffee addict, eventually phasing out soda entirely.

The pleasant aroma was the one thing going for him this morning. He spent the late morning hours sorting through the cabinets. With so much time having passed since the last visit, he suspected there to be a few expired items. For the most part, the cabinets stored spices. There were so many to choose from. Hayden didn't even know what some of them were used for, but up until now, he never cared. His beloved Mary knew precisely how to use each and every one. The evidence was in every single meal she prepared.

Once again, Hayden felt a pang of regret for coming here. What was meant to take his mind off his grief only made him dwell on it more. Slowly, he realized there was no running away from his sorrow. Not even the beauty of nature could allay the reality that was now his life.

He was a lone father with two kids who had no direction in life.

Hayden closed the cabinet doors. To his surprise, most of the items there were well within the expiration date. Mary did not purchase any spices or ingredients willy nilly. She only bought items she had a purpose for, leading to everything getting used and promptly replaced.

With nothing else to do, he double-checked the fridge. The vegetables and lunch meat were in their proper places. The only thing lacking was beer. Hayden was not much of a drinker. He would have a beer every so often if he was in a social environment that called for it, but his consumption was generally limited to that.

Today, though, a dose of alcohol didn't sound so bad.

An inner voice warned him against what he was considering. Almost every man in America had heard at least one story of someone who medicated with alcohol. It never went well in the long run.

Hayden glanced at his two sons. As usual, they were sprawled out on the furniture, entranced with their handheld units. Even after numerous suggestions to go outside and enjoy the sunshine, their actions made it clear they would rather stay indoors and rot their brains out.

"How 'bout we go out on the boat?" he said. Per what was now the new usual, he had to repeat himself in order to get a response. "Hey! Guys?" Finally, their eyes moved in his direction. "How 'bout we go out on the boat?"

"Eh, maybe later," Franklin said. Billy did not offer a response.

That settled it. Hayden grabbed his keys and went out the door. "I'm gonna make a run to the gas station and see if it's open. Will you guys be alright here by yourselves?"

"See if they have charging cables while you're there," Franklin said.

Hayden felt his teeth grinding. Of course, the brat couldn't even add a 'please' to his demand.

"And headphones," Billy said. "I couldn't find mine."

"Fine. Stay inside until I get back. I won't be long." Hayden stepped out into the sunlight and shut the door behind him. He gave a long look at the clouds and attempted to imagine what Heaven looked like. Again, what was meant to bring comfort only sparked sorrow and bitterness. "If I could trade places with you, I would."

He stepped into his pickup truck and started the engine. He put the vehicle in reverse and started to back out.

"Whoa!"

Hayden hit the brakes, stopping just short of colliding with a large eight-pointer. It seemingly materialized out of nowhere, darting past his tailgate before disappearing into a section of forest behind his cabin.

Before he knew it, another deer appeared, running in the same direction and with the same urgency. Other animals appeared in its wake, each one bolting to the east and south as though the devil was right behind them.

Hayden put the truck in park and rolled down the window. His heart leapt into his throat at the horrid sound of some bellowing beast. There was no doubt in his mind that beast was one of the grizzlies he saw earlier. Except now, it was unmistakably pissed off.

Its howls were loud and constant, with fluctuations in its pitch as it engaged in whatever struggle it was in.

Questions naturally flooded Hayden's mind. Did the two bears get into a tussle? Was there a third bear in the vicinity that didn't get along with them? Could one of them be a female and receiving some unwanted 'attention' from the other?

He stepped out of the truck and listened, keeping one hand on his pistol. His concentration was broken by the sound of the front door opening. Franklin and Billy stepped out, both alarmed by the disturbing howl.

"Dad?" Billy said, making sure to stay behind his brother.

"Is that a bear?" Franklin asked.

Hayden moved to the front porch. "Yeah. It sounds like it."

"What's going on?" Franklin asked. "Why is it making that noise?"

Hayden chuckled in an attempt to put the nervous boy at ease. "Oh, it's probably nothing. There were two bears out there. They're probably scrabbling over some berries or…"

The howl elevated to a very unnatural high pitch. Hayden could not fathom what was going on. The only mental image he could muster was that the bear was in tremendous pain—the kind one felt when every bone in its body was slowly being crushed.

Following an intense sound of snapping branches, the howling ceased. A brief silence flooded the woods before a new sound emerged. Heavy footsteps drummed the forest floor, rapidly intensifying as they neared the property.

"Get in the cabin," Hayden said.

"But what's going on?" Billy asked.

"I don't know, but just—"

From the tree line came the second grizzly. Its fur frizzled and its jaws bared, it gave one look at the humans and bellowed.

If it wasn't already obvious the thing was agitated, it was now. Hayden pushed his kids inside the cabin and grabbed the cannister of repellent off the kitchen countertop.

"Move!" he shouted at the boys as he returned to the porch. He put himself in front of them and aimed the spray at the bear. "Hey! Hey! Hey, you! Get out of here!"

The bear snarled once, only to shut its jaws and look over its shoulder. From the woods on the west property came a current of grinding dirt and uprooting vegetation.

Hayden, though face-to-face with an angry nine-foot grizzly, found himself staring at the woods. Something *huge* was coming. Not huge in the sense of a full-grown bear, but more to the scale of a freight train plowing through the forest.

The bear grunted, no longer interested in the human, but in its own safety. It turned left to retreat to the north area of forest leading to Jack's cabin, only to stop after reaching the tree line.

Both the bear and Hayden noticed how the grinding sound had hooked around the property, intercepting the large mammal. Flustered and confused, the grizzly resorted to its most primal means of defense. It stood on its hind legs, held its enormous paws out, and bellowed a challenge to the unseen assailant.

It came to regret that action.

From the forest floor rose a massive, limbless form. Flexible as a garden hose, the fiend bent its head to gaze down at the grizzly.

"Dad?!" Franklin's voice came out as a croak. His throat had tightened to the point of suppressing his voice.

Hayden's did the same. "Stay back!"

Adrenaline shook his limbs and supercharged his heart rate. His bowels threatened to let loose right then and there. Had he not relieved himself minutes earlier, his bladder would undoubtedly have spilt its contents through his jeans. The rush of blood made him feel mildly lightheaded. Moreover, he questioned his sanity.

How could one not when finding himself staring at a gargantuan *snake*!

Razor-tipped spines adorned the black stripes lining its dark-green body. Its head was narrow, almost crocodilian, but retaining the distinct features of a serpent.

Its size did not hinder its speed. The titanic snake struck the grizzly with the same lightning-fast motion of an everyday rattlesnake.

The grizzly howled and bellowed, first feeling the needle-shaped fangs penetrating its flesh, then spun as its captor worked several meters of body length around its furry torso.

Bones, containing ten times the mineral content of humans, snapped like toothpicks under the intense pressure. The bear reared its head back, parted its jaws, and let loose a dying howl. Its tongue stuck straight into the sky as though trying to escape the horror the rest of the body was subjected to.

With a horrid *SNAP*, the bear went limp. The snake uncoiled, letting its victim drop onto the grass, its spine broken, ribs splintered, and internal organs squished.

Without a moment of delay, it set its sights on the humans.

"Get inside!" Hayden yelled to his kids. Franklin grabbed Billy by the shoulders and yanked him into the living room.

The snake jerked its head, detecting their movements. In a single burst of movement, it 'swam' across the lawn, quickly reaching the front door.

"No! No! No!" Hayden's worst nightmare was coming true before his very eyes. As much as he loved the woods, there was always a fear of his kids getting mauled by some wild animal.

In the blink of an eye, his imagination ran through a hundred different scenarios, all of which made him want to vomit. Each outcome drew him to the same conclusion: This was worse than his worst nightmares.

Hayden knew snakes well enough to know they ate their prey whole. Considering the size of his kids and that of its mouth, it probably would not even bother crushing them. It would just bite down and swallow them whole.

The thought of his young boys trapped, alive and terrified, in the depths of its gullet sparked a simultaneous feeling of panic and determination Hayden never thought possible.

In his split-second of planning, he did the only thing he could think of. He aimed the bear repellent spray and delivered a chemical stream at the side of the creature's head.

The serpent whipped its head back, curving its upper body into a vertical S shape as it tried to shake the strange substance loose.

"Dad?!" Franklin yelled out from inside the cabin. "Dad? Where are you?!"

"Franklin! Billy! Get in the cellar. Get in there and do not come out! I'll come back for you! Just get in!"

Hayden prayed that, for once in their lives, his kids would listen to him. Their lives literally depended on it.

He backed away as he spoke, watching the snake shake the last of the repellent from its eye. It pointed its head at him, seeing him as both food and a nuisance. Hayden pointed his cannister and depressed the lever. A small stream jetted from the nozzle, followed by an empty hiss of air.

Hayden glanced at the now-useless repellent, cursed under his breath, and tossed it aside. Glimpsing over his shoulder, he saw his boat and dock. With no other options, he turned on his heel and sprinted.

He could hear the grinding of scaly flesh against the dirt behind him, quickly closing the distance. With it clear there was no hope of getting his boat started on time, Hayden dove under the dock.

He was in the water now, crouched in the shallows and looking up through the planks. The snake's head arrived on the other side, tilting down to gaze at him with its yellow eye.

Now, the image of *himself* being swallowed alive was front and center in Hayden's mind.

He drew his pistol, put it between the planks, and fired a shot into the snake's eye.

The creature reared its head back and parted its jaws. Its upper body slashed the air in a display of rage and pain.

Hayden quivered beneath the dock. Not only was the thing not going away, but it was very, *very* pissed off.

A fact evidenced by its next action.

The snake slammed its head onto the dock. An explosive impact reduced the structure to a series of wood scraps.

Hayden found himself on his back, fully submerged in the river. The dock broke apart on top of him, shaking the pistol from his hand. The field of debris that was once his dock began floating down the river. The wooden legs were still intact, keeping him from being swept away.

Through the water and silt, he could see the snake arching its body over the water. A forked tongue flicked, its tips tapping the water's surface. The sensory receptors picked up a hundred scents from a hundred different sources throughout the river.

Fish, crayfish, invertebrates, amphibians, and a lone submerged human.

Realizing it was about to snatch him out of the water, Hayden let go of the dock leg and rolled to his left. The snake struck, its head embedding in the riverbed where he had lain a half-second prior.

He rose to his feet and drew a breath. With the river current at his back, he moved forward in the shallows in a desperate effort to gain distance between himself and the snake.

A few steps in front of him was his boat. It had drifted south after the dock was destroyed, only to get lodged against the riverbed. He made his way over to it and threw himself aboard.

Now on his knees, he leaned over the outboard motor and grabbed the ripcord.

"Oh, please God, let this work."

He yanked.

Apparently, the big man upstairs was not willing to lend a hand in this particular moment. The engine turned over once, but refused to come to life.

Hayden turned and looked at the curving figure towering above him. The snake dislodged its head from the mushy riverbed and poised for another strike.

"Oh, God…" Hayden closed his eyes and awaited his fate.

The sound of a motor reached his ears. It was not his, but one farther up the river, gradually getting closer.

He opened his eyes and looked past the beast. Several meters up the river was a twenty-four-foot pontoon boat. At its helm was a bewildered Jack Tracy.

The snake hooked its head to look in the direction of the noise, sparking fear in the man's eyes.

Hayden waved his arms. "Jack! Turn around! Get out of here!"

Jack Tracy had been testing his recently repaired motor and had decided to cast a few lines on the river. He was in the middle of reeling in a twenty-inch trout when he heard shouting, howling, and the unmistakable sound of a gunshot coming from Hayden Spencer's cabin.

Remembering his neighbor's warning about grizzlies being in the area, he decided to cut the line and speed over to Hayden's property. He had a 357. revolver strapped to his hip. He never left the cabin without it. Out here, it could be foolish to do so.

Jack made his way around the bend, hearing a crashing noise as he neared Hayden's property.

He was not prepared for what he saw. At worst, he expected to see an angry grizzly tearing things up in the yard. What he saw was far worse.

A colossal snake elevated its head on the shoreline, bearing down on a twelve-foot aluminum boat. Hayden was on the aft seat, waving his arms and shouting at him. Jack did not register the warning, for his eyes were transfixed on the leviathan.

The creature turned its head in his direction and flicked its tongue. Two yellow eyes expressed murderous intent, the left one leaking blood.

"Oh, dear Lord!"

Jack cocked the hammer on his revolver and discharged a shot at its head. The snake twitched, having caught the bullet square on the nose. The thick, gravely skin deflected the bullet, as well as the five that followed.

Regretting his decision to stand his ground, Jack engaged the throttle and hooked the wheel all the way to the left.

Midway through his about-turn, the snake came at him. Large swells traveled the width of the river, making way for a hundred-and-thirty feet of pure muscle.

Panic took hold of the outdoorsman. Desperate, he squeezed the trigger of his revolver, despite knowing all six cartridges were spent.

The snake's head struck the starboard hull like a battering ram against castle doors. Aluminum, plastic, and fiberglass split apart. The boat capsized, sending its occupant into the water.

Jack quickly surfaced and fought against the current, only to be forced southward. No matter how hard he swam, the river pushed him back, as though deliberately assisting the snake.

Much to his regret, he looked over his shoulder to gauge the distance between himself and the predator.

That distance turned out to be about five inches.

It was level with the river's surface, jaws hyperextended.

"NOOO!!!"

The next thing Jack saw was darkness.

"Oh, Jesus! Oh, God!"

Hayden dry-heaved after witnessing a bulge that was Jack Tracy run down the snake's throat. His feet were still kicking as the snake gulped him down. A soulless beast lacking even a hint of compassion, it did not bother killing its victims if it didn't have to. It was perfectly content with swallowing people alive.

And he was next.

Hayden grabbed the ripcord and gave it another go. Again, the engine failed to start.

"Come on, damn you!"

He yanked.

The motor sputtered, then roared.

"YES!" He looked up. The snake was slithering up the river. Right toward him. "SHIT!"

He put his foot against the shoreline and boosted his ride from the riverbed. Twisting the handle, he put the motor in third gear and raced south.

The snake wiggled its body, acting like an enormous fin to keep up with the small boat. Hayden could not believe it. The thing was not giving up. One mile turned into two. Then three.

All the while, the snake gradually narrowed the distance.

One thought brought him comfort. He was leading the creature away from his kids.

"Please, God, don't let them leave the cellar." The next prayer was for his own safety. One fact was plain: it would take a miracle for him to survive this. "And God, if you can spare any guardian angels, now would be a good time to send them."

CHAPTER 8

Thomas knew it was a waste of time to peek inside the crushed cabin, but as he technically was a first responder, he decided to play it safe. When they first arrived on the property, all four team members knew there were no survivors. The two-story cabin had essentially imploded and the only vehicle on site had been tossed across the lawn like a tennis ball. The only tire treads in the area matched those on the truck, suggesting the property owners did not escape in a second vehicle.

That did not mean the ground was not marked. Something had traveled in a zig-zag trajectory, flattening and uprooting much of the landscape. The inside of the cabin contained nothing but scattered belongings, dangling ceiling components, and all sorts of wreckage.

Thomas quickly backed away. It was a miracle the building had not collapsed in on itself. He turned around and joined Charity by the wrecked truck.

"Nobody?" she asked. The question was as much of a formality as Thomas' effort to check the interior.

"No." He glanced at Howard, who was busy using his tablet to monitor his three drones. "Anything yet?"

Howard turned his head, just enough to see the Captain in his peripheral vision. "Why yes! I just decided to keep it to myself the entire time!"

Thomas nodded. "Touché."

Archer arrived from the other side of the cabin, having conducted a thorough check of the surrounding area. "Nobody nearby. Organism moved off into the west where it burrowed into another tunnel."

"Any idea where it leads?" Thomas asked. Archer pointed south. Right toward the entrance near the marker Corporal Lamont had set up. The Captain quickly put the pieces together. Lamont's team continued their search of the area and came across this cabin. Afterwards, they heard the C4 explosions and ran back to the tunnel. From there, they retreated to their IFAV, only to get intercepted by *something*.

Thomas looked to Charity. "What do you make of this? Obviously, we're dealing with a mutation. The question is what got mutated, if not a bug?"

"Well, let's go with what we know," Charity said. "You're looking at the same thing I am. That cabin was not torn apart, but crushed from an outside force. All four walls appear to have had an equal amount of pressure, meaning it was not impacted, but *compressed*."

"You're suggesting something constricted this building?" Thomas said.

"You tell me," Charity replied, gesturing at the damage.

Thomas crossed his arms and studied the nature of the destruction. He had no counterargument. Everything Charity had said was accurate.

"Okay, but what could do that? I'm not aware of Wyoming being home to many snakes. Animals like boa constrictors tend to be far south of us. And I don't see any pet shops nearby."

"No, but Wyoming does have a species called the eastern racer," Charity said. An intrigued Thomas Rodney raised his eyebrows. He was all ears. "Their scientific name is Coluber constrictor. Normal ones can move up to ten miles per hour. Their common names depend on their color. There are brown racers, black racers, green, blue, tan."

"How big do they normally get?" Thomas asked.

"It varies, but many can reach nearly sixty inches in length," she replied.

Thomas inhaled through clenched teeth, glaring at the crushed cabin. "If an inch-long hornet can turn into four-foot monstrosities, I'd hate to see what a five-foot snake could turn into."

"What about the holes, though?" Howard asked. "Can snakes do that?"

"Sure, absolutely they can," Charity said. "Generally, they only do it through loose soil. Racers generally do it to lay their eggs. However, if that's what we're dealing with, we're talking about a creature with enough strength to plow through concrete, no problem. Tunnelling underground, depending on the density of the forest and any rock formations, probably would not be a problem for a snake of a hundred-plus feet in length."

"Fabulous," Thomas said. He instinctively started looking at the ground and listening for any kind of vibration. There was no telling where its present location was. Out here, searching for a creature, even one as large as Charity suggested, would be like looking for a needle in a haystack. Making matters worse, Renee and the chopper squadron were heading northeast in pursuit of the hornet princess. He needed a bird's eye view.

With that in mind, he glanced at Howard's monitor. There were three different screens relaying the signals from the three drones. All three of them displayed sections of forest.

"Still nothing, Captain," Howard said. "Except trees, of course. They're maintaining a three-mile search grid."

"Expand it," Thomas said. "Let's assume it's not on the move. Maybe it's resting somewhere. Charity? What kind of habitat would eastern racers slumber in when they're not hunting?"

"Grassy areas," Charity said. "That's what normal ones like, at least. If this thing is a snake, and it's as big as we suspect, it might seek out a sparser area of forest. It might also be attracted to a water source. Not sure if there's any lakes or ponds nearby, but there is the river."

"I'll have one of the drones travel the length of the river," Howard said. He tapped a few keys on his module to provide new instructions to his drones. "Hopefully Renee kills that hornet so she can lend her eyes to the search. My drones can only do so much on their own."

"Doubting your machines, Howard?" Thomas said.

"No. That's what you do," Howard replied.

"Oh, geez. Heeere we go." Thomas turned away, disinterested in another remark about how he prevented Howard's rover from eliminating the hornet colony's upper chamber. "How about you make your devices a little less fragile? They don't do much good if a love tap from a bug can disable them."

"It was more than a love tap, but fair enough," Howard said. "Keep in mind, we're dealing with organisms with vast strength. A 'love tap' from a hornet could potentially burst your skull. But to your point, I'm in the middle of developing several projects that'll help us eliminate the threats. Especially the bigger ones."

Thomas chuckled at that last sentence. "The bigger ones? You make it sound like you're trying to construct building-sized robots to fight some of these monsters."

Howard remained quiet, answering Thomas with a look that hinted accuracy in his statement.

Thomas' grin vanished. "Wait, that *is* what you're trying to do?"

Even Charity snorted. "It's been a dream project of his since G.O.R.E. Sector was founded."

"It's a work in progress," Howard said. "It takes a lot of testing. You think it's easy putting together a fully functional, completely agile mechanical robot of that size that can take a licking and keep on ticking?"

"No," Charity said. "Exactly why I feel it's a waste of time. You're better off putting those resources into weapons research. Why General Kilmore bothers entertaining the thought at all is beyond me."

"He likes thinking outside the box," Howard replied. "That's why he thinks I'm the most valuable member of the team."

All eyes turned toward him.

Archer sported a grin and shook his head. "Bullshit."

"Uh-huh, right," Charity added.

Thomas, unsure if the 'hurt' look on Howard's face was genuine or sarcastic, decided to keep his remark to himself. Instead, he went with "He seriously said that?"

Howard shrugged. "Okay, no. But it's obviously the case. At least, to me it is."

"Wait, weren't you the one who supplied his office with new computers and monitors?" Charity said.

Howard pointed a finger at her. "Hey, those worked perfectly fine."

"Oh, sure. As long as you didn't need them to turn on, or not freeze up, or blow a fuse."

"That was the prototype," Howard said. "The second batch worked perfectly… Oh, to hell with you jerks." While the team laughed, Howard turned his eyes to the monitor. "Just you wait. One of these days, my inventions will save your asses and when it does, I'm going to do a victory dance right in your faces. And you guys will think twice before…"

He froze, motionlessly staring at the screen.

Thomas leaned forward. "Let me guess. Your drones are malfunctioning."

An anxious Howard aimed the screen at him. "Quite the opposite! Dr. Black was right! Here's our snake!"

Charity and Archer assembled alongside the Captain and took in the view of a dark green squiggly shape coursing down the river.

Right away, they learned the reptilian was not going for a luxury swim. Just a few yards in front of it was a twelve-foot aluminum boat with a single occupant on board.

"Oh, hell," Thomas said.

Charity measured the creature's size against the boat. "Son of a bitch. It's at least a hundred and ten feet long."

"And it's on the hunt. Mount up!" Thomas ordered. All at once, the team hopped into their Growler. "So much for catching the thing off guard. Howard, have your drone keep pace with the thing. You said they have nine-millimeter rounds?"

"That's correct," Howard said.

"Get the other two birds over there and put 'em to use. Get that bastard off that poor guy's back. Charity, now will be a good time to drive like a freak."

In direct response, she floored the accelerator and went east.

CHAPTER 9

"Go away! GO AWAY! Get away from me!"

The shreds of bravery and stoicism that enabled Hayden Spencer to lure the snake away from his kids was long gone. All that remained was sheer terror and desperation. Having witnessed the death of Jack Tracy, he knew precisely what fate awaited him should he be caught by the serpent.

A true devilish fiend, it kept its eyes fixed on him, boring an unforgettable image into the mind of its prey. The creature, which had already consumed its neighbor and left the crushed corpse of a grizzly bear in his front lawn, had pursued him for three miles and showed no sign of giving up.

Hayden could not help but question if the snake was chasing him out of hunger or if it got some sick thrill. He pushed the throttle to the max, praying his pursuer would get bored and give up. His imagination conjured up horrific images of being slurped down a wet, slimy esophagus and ending up in a dark, hot dungeon where he would be melted by stomach acid. Sensations of flesh peeling off his bones induced a need to dry heave.

Hayden swallowed and resumed the chase. He considered making a sharp turn for either one of the shorelines, but knew the snake would be on top of him before he could set foot ashore. He was screwed. His only option was an equally futile one. Keep going downriver and hope the snake would give up.

Up until now, he had taken life for granted. Even after the death of his beloved Mary and knowing life could end at any moment, he still assumed he would live to be eighty and die peacefully of natural causes.

He glanced over his shoulder.

The snake flicked its forked tongue. The dual tips were just a few feet away. The creature, getting close to striking range, doubled the intensity of its movements. Its squiggly body produced a series of waves that traveled to both shorelines.

If that wasn't bad enough, Hayden took in the sounds of a clunking engine. The motor stalled, bringing his retreat to an end.

He glared at the machine, resentful of its lack of stamina. Then came a wave of anger directed at himself for failing to perform maintenance on it. He knew the outboard was old and needed some attention. Like with many things in his life, he put it off. Then again, he never thought his life would literally depend on it.

"No! NO!"

Water dripped into the river as the serpent raised its head. Twenty feet of neck cocked back like a hammer, the head quivering, ready to snap its jaws.

Hayden clenched his teeth, his worst fears milliseconds away from becoming reality.

BANG! BANG! BANG! BANG! BANG!

The snake jerked to the side, then turned its eyes at the pesky machine hovering over its head. Buzzing like a mosquito powered by dual rotors, the thing had darted out of the trees, apparently determined to do battle with the monster.

Hayden traded glances, watching both the monster and the flying machine. The latter had a slight buzzing sound as it darted over the river. Like a moth over a flame, it darted back and forth, never holding position for more than a few seconds. Underneath its body was a glassy circular frame which Hayden, after a few moments of observation, determined to be a camera lens. The second object, protruding from under its 'nose' was some kind of small metal barrel.

Flashes from its muzzle, accompanied by loud cracks of noise, confirmed it to be a gun.

The thing was some kind of aerial combat drone. Hayden did not bother wasting time wondering where it came from or why it was here. All that mattered was that he had a fresh opportunity to get out of here.

He tried to start the motor again, to no avail. After the third yank of the cord, he resorted to paddling water with his bare hands, gradually angling the boat to the west shore.

Behind him, the snake was raising its head, twitching as bullets struck its flesh. It snapped its jaws at the sky, its many rows of needle-shaped teeth briefly visible. The drone zipped to the east, avoiding their clutches. Another couple of gunshots struck the creature's neck, failing to pierce its flesh, but succeeding in distracting it.

Though its attention was no longer on Hayden, his troubles continued to mount. The snake performed a full three-sixty-degree turn to pursue the drone. As it did, its tail lashed across the river's surface. Its tip struck the boat, knocking it and its owner out of the water like golf balls.

Hayden splashed down in the shallows, his boat bouncing bow over stern on the shoreline. Dazed and confused, but still remembering the terrifying threat behind him, he forced himself to paddle. After a few moments, his fingertips touched the mucky silt comprising the riverbed.

He pulled himself onto the muddy shore, then lifted himself to his hands and knees. Like an awkwardly-shaped wild animal, he scampered several feet from the water.

A splash of water trickled on his back. He turned around just in time to see the snake lifting its head fifty feet into the sky. The drone was no longer firing its weapon, despite the target only being a few meters away.

It attempted to move to the side in an attempt to avoid a strike. Only this time, the snake anticipated this move and altered the angle of attack.

A mechanical *crunch* echoed across the sky. Pieces of metal trickled from the snake's jaws into the river.

The beast tightened its jaws, crushing its prey until all 'life' had fled its mechanical body, then tossed it to the side. The many pieces of the drone separated as they spiraled into the eastern shore.

Out of nowhere, one of the pieces of debris exploded. The snake whirled away from the blast area, flabbergasted at the intensity and randomness. The shockwave reached Hayden, stalling him further.

The snake watched the direction of the blast, waiting for any other random surprises. It yawned repeatedly, ridding itself of the tiny flakes of plastic and metal that remained. Satisfied the danger was over, it bent its neck to look at Hayden.

He sprang to his feet and retreated into the forest. The weight of his soaking wet clothes slowed him down. Physical and mental fatigue added to his setbacks, as did the ringing in his ears due to the explosion. The ill-timed combination of adrenaline and exhaustion resulted in clumsiness.

He only made it a few yards into the woods before tripping over a broken branch. Now on his back, he turned his eyes to the river. Sure enough, the snake was still intent on chasing him.

Its speed, even in the water, tripled his own. In no time, it was slithering across the shore and through the woods until reaching its target. Once again, it was ready to strike, only to get distracted by another mechanical disturbance. This time, the intrusion was not airborne, but terrestrial.

Thick rubber tires crunched vegetation and rotting twigs. The sound of tires ceased in a grinding motion as brakes were applied. Boots hit the ground, going in opposite directions.

Hayden turned to look behind him. Twenty feet from his left shoulder was a green military-style light utility vehicle. Four personnel had just stepped off of it, all of whom wore black tactical outfits. Three of them held military-style assault rifles. What kind they were, Hayden was unsure, for he was untrained in such things. All he did know was that the fourth guy was clearly armed with some kind of large sniper rifle.

Moving alongside him was the leader of the group.

"Hot damn, that's a big ass snake! Howard, Charity, keep to the left. Careful, its attention is on you right now."

"Yeah, I've noticed!" the one named Charity replied. "You had a golden opportunity, Howard. You could've detonated the drone while it was still in its mouth."

"Wasn't my fault," the man named Howard said. "It tossed the drone right before the charge detonated."

The leader turned to the man with the sniper rifle. "You got explosive rounds in that magazine, Archer?" The sniper nodded. "Good. Do what you do best." The leader turned his eyes to Hayden. "I recommend covering your ears, sir."

Hayden did not waste time complying.

The man named Archer pointed his rifle and squeezed the trigger. The explosive round struck the snake right in the throat, knocking it backward. Archer fired again, this time hitting it somewhere in the center of its coiling body. The snake squirmed like a worm on a hook, its body looping behind the curtain of smoke.

Two more explosive rounds struck its hide before the serpent slithered toward the riverside.

"Howard!" the team leader shouted. "Use your drones. Keep tabs on the bastard."

"Already on it." Howard immediately tapped the screen of a tablet. A pair of drones, identical to the first one that appeared over the river, pursued the snake.

Hayden uncovered his ears and watched the beast enter the water. The team ran past him, guns pointed, ready to finish the fight. Hayden, figuring the safest place was behind them, decided to follow.

They converged on the shoreline and watched as the snake disappeared into the woods across the river.

"Still got a visual," Howard said. The leader glanced at the screen.

Hayden stood on his tiptoes to do the same. Sure enough, the cameras under the drones displayed the dark-green line moving across the ground.

His eyes went to the patches on their shoulders. G.O.R.E. Sector.

Son of a bitch. It's THEM!

"It stopped!" Howard said. The creature on the screen was looping its lower half, while bending its upper body like a fishhook, pressing its snout against the ground. In a twisting motion, it successfully dug a hole into the earth. With each passing foot, it gained momentum.

"It's burrowing," Charity said.

After a few moments, the snake vanished, leaving a five-foot crater in its wake.

"Visual lost," Howard confirmed.

The leader lifted a radio to his lips. "Guard One?"

"Go ahead."

"Target is subterranean. Be extra careful."

"Copy that. We heard the explosions all the way from here. I'm guessing this means you didn't manage to kill it."

"Negative. Target has armored skin." The leader gave a glance to the ravaged section of forest where the snake had been when Archer shot it. "Doesn't even look like we drew blood."

"Looks like we'll need heavier artillery. Want us to meet in the same place?"

The leader thought for a moment. "Standby for an update."

"Standing by."

"I can continue monitoring the area, Thomas," Howard said.

"Negative. It could be anywhere by now. We need to mobilize." The leader, whose name had finally been revealed, turned to face Hayden. "Looks like you could use a ride."

Hayden smirked. "I wouldn't complain." A million questions formed a massive list in his brain. Many of them were answered with his observations, previous news broadcasts, and simple common sense.

Monsters were real. G.O.R.E. Sector was hunting them. These guys were either a strike team or a reconnaissance party, or both. The third option was most likely, considering the titles on their badges and the weaponry they carried.

"You guys saved my life. Thank you."

"No need for that," Thomas said. "I'm Captain Thomas Rodney. We're Raptor Pack, part of…"

"G.O.R.E. Sector," Hayden said, still catching his breath. "I heard of you guys. I thought it was a bunch of government conspiracy nonsense."

"I wish it were the case," Charity said.

"You guys were already in the area," Hayden said. "Were you aware that thing was out here?"

Thomas shook his head. "No. We were destroying a new hornet nest several miles east of here. I'm guessing you didn't receive the warnings."

"No." Hayden tensed. *That's why the gas station was closed.* "The damn mountains in the area screw with radio and cell signals."

"I see. Regardless, while we were dealing with the bugs, we lost contact with one of our scout teams. Sadly, it appears they encountered the snake. We need to track it and find it before it kills anyone else. We tried to evacuate, but as you mentioned, not everyone received the broadcast. Do you know if there's anyone else residing in this region?"

"It already killed my neighbor," Hayden said. A new wave of adrenaline nearly lifted him off the ground. "My kids! I have a cabin a few miles north of here! My boys are there. The snake attacked, I got in the boat and led it downriver."

Thomas took him by the shoulder and directed him to the Growler. "We'll go there right now." As the team assembled by the vehicle, he grabbed ahold of his radio. "Raptor Pack to Command Central, is there any update on Falcon and Eagle Squadron?"

"Still tracking the princess," a deep, commanding voice replied.

"Copy that, General," Thomas said. "Please redirect them west of the river when they're done. We've got a new target. Snake. Black and green in color, over a hundred feet in length, capable of burrowing under the ground. We've rounded up a civilian and are heading north to a cabin property he owns. Guard One, we have our new meeting area…"

CHAPTER 10

The cellar was dark and moist, full of mostly empty shelves and some spare tools in the back corner. It was there where Billy and Franklin chose to huddle. The former held a hammer and a screwdriver, watching the stairway intently. Franklin held an old handsaw. It was dull and rusted, but it was better than nothing.

Since the attack, they had hardly moved. It was partially out of fear for their lives. Not every day did somebody get to experience getting attacked by a monster snake.

There was another fear bolting them to this dungeon, one neither wanted to speak of. They could hear the sound of rampaging in the dock area and river. Sounds of gunfire gave them momentary hope that the snake had been killed, only to have it stripped away when they heard screaming and what sounded like the smashing of a large object. Being on a river, it was probably a boat.

The marathon of chaos ended with the sound of a motor going downriver, followed by heavy sounds of splashing. It didn't take much imagination to know their dad retreated in the motorboat. What they didn't know was his fate.

Franklin groaned as his brother shifted against him for the hundredth time.

"Hold still, you dweeb!" he hissed.

"I can't help it," Billy whispered. "My arm hurts. It really hurts." He tucked his left arm close.

Franklin sighed. His brother was always a pretty spry kid. Even as a toddler, he rarely tripped and fell. Whenever going up or down a flight of stairs, Billy often took three steps at a time, much to Mom and Dad's dismay. Never once did he miscalculate a step.

Until his life depended on it, that is.

He was two-thirds down the cellar stairway when he lost his footing. Down he went, his forearm hitting the edge of the bottom stair. He didn't appear too hurt at first, probably due to the adrenaline.

As time went on, he began to complain of the discomfort in his forearm. Eventually, it got to the point where making a fist was painful.

Billy shifted again. "It hurts."

Franklin bit his lip, not wanting to deal with this issue. "I know."

"I really have to pee."

"Are you…" Franklin clenched his teeth, preventing himself from shouting. He took a deep breath and lowered his voice. "Are you serious?"

"Yes."

"Then go to the bathroom," Franklin said.

"I don't want to. It's upstairs." Billy tucked his head down and squeezed his eyes shut.

Franklin tilted his head away and sighed. "Then go in the corner."

"No! That's gross," Billy said.

A smug look of astonishment came over his older brother. Franklin scooted back as far as he could, preferring the edge of a nearby shelf pressing against his shoulder to the pesky budging from Billy.

"There's a snake the size of *Godzilla* out there trying to eat us, and you're concerned about the sanitary nature of peeing in the corner?" He gestured at the surrounding cellar. "Take a look around. The place is full of rust. Dad let this place go to rot."

"He said he'd fix it," Billy said.

"Yeah? Well, he didn't," Franklin replied. "And now, he dragged us out here to get killed by that thing."

"He didn't know that snake was out there."

"Yeah, fine. Maybe." Franklin turned his head to hide his own whimpering expression. "Doesn't matter anyway. You see how he is when he speaks to us. He doesn't care."

Billy bumped him in the leg with his hammer. "Shut up."

"You shut up." Franklin retaliated by bumping him back.

"Dad was going to fix this place, but Mom got sick." A teary-eyed Billy pointed a finger in Franklin's face. "If you paid attention and kept your face out of your Nintendo Switch, you'd know this."

"Oh, you're one to talk!" Franklin said. "I seem to remember your thumbs peddling some joysticks. Like it matters now. Dad's probably dead, and nobody's coming to save us."

"Dad's not dead. Shut up," Billy said.

"You saw it," Franklin said. "It chased him right to the dock. It probably got him right there."

"No! I heard the motor," Billy said.

"Then it chased him," Franklin said. Little by little, his charade of indifference began to break apart. "He ran away, down the river… with the snake chasing him." A tear broke free. "It was about to get us, but Dad made it chase him instead. And I don't know if he got away or not."

Billy dropped the screwdriver. It hurt too much to hold it in his left hand. Trembling from the pain, he moved closer to his brother. This time, Franklin did not nudge him away or complain.

"I miss Mom."

"Yeah." Franklin wiped his face clean. "Me too. It's not fair. First, she dies, now we might've lost Dad. We don't have anyone left."

"You have me," Billy said.

Franklin scoffed. "Yeah, that'll get me far in life."

"It did in March, when we beat Basil and Johnny during their *Halo* livestream. I went back and watched the views. I think two-thousand people watched that."

That memory got a small grin from his older brother.

"Yeah, we did kick their butts," Franklin said. "Their reaction was priceless."

"And who scored the most points?" Billy said.

Franklin gave him a bitter look. "Yeah, okay, fine. You did." They shared a much-needed chuckle. It was a good memory which brought some brief, but welcome levity to their current predicament. "But don't forget who was key to us winning Jamie's *Super Smash Bros Ultimate* tournament."

"Donkey Kong?" Billy asked.

"No. Me! Jerk."

Billy chuckled, then frowned. "We haven't played together much. You're always doing your thing, I'm always doing mine."

"I guess things have changed," Franklin replied. "With Mom dying and Dad being depressed... I don't know. It's not fair." A few moments of silence passed. "Maybe, if we get out of this, we'll host our very own livestream. Maybe we'll do a *Halo* playthrough, or something. Use the publicity we gained from Basil's audience."

Billy perked up at the idea. "Okay." It was a struggle to maintain that newfound positive energy, especially with the pain in his arm. More importantly, they were still trapped in the cellar, not knowing what ultimately happened to their father, and unsure if it was even safe. "I hope Dad's okay."

Franklin, forcing aside his pessimism, put a hand on Billy's shoulder. "I think he's alright."

"You think so?"

"Yeah. You said it yourself. He went downriver on his boat. The snake is big. Maybe it can't swim for very long. Dad knows the river pretty well."

Billy nodded. "Okay." He winced. "I really have to pee. I don't want to go in the corner."

Franklin groaned. "Then go upstairs."

"I'm scared to. Will you come with me?" Billy asked. Franklin gulped. Billy shifted in place, barely holding it in. "Pleeeeease."

"But what if that thing's up—" Franklin squeezed his eyes shut. For the first time in forever, he asked himself what would make his father happy. The answer was simple. 'Think about others.' He stood up. "Let's move quietly."

"Thank you!" Billy got up and hugged him with his good arm.

"Shh!" Despite the harshness in his voice, Franklin gently hugged him back. "Alright, let's go."

Together, the boys ascended the stairs. Each step was taken with caution. Every creak in the panels made them shudder. The natural sunlight at the top of the stairway was both welcome and ominous. As far as they knew, that snake was right outside the door, waiting for them.

Billy had his hammer tightly gripped and raised high. Franklin was right behind him, holding the sawblade like a sword.

Billy's bladder urged him to quicken his pace. Giving in, he took the final few steps in two large strides. Franklin sprinted to keep up. If this was it, they might as well get it over with.

They arrived in the hallway, grunting like warriors from their favorite fantasy adventures. They found nothing but silence in the hallway and living room. Franklin went forward and inspected the front of the cabin. Everything was intact. The yard was empty, save for the dead grizzly. From what he could see, the snake was nowhere to be found.

Next came the part he dreaded most. Franklin debated if he wanted to know the answer to this unspoken question, and concluded not knowing was worse. He moved to the front door and looked to the dock.

The dock was smashed, but the boat was gone.

Billy cleared his throat. "Is Dad…?"

"He's not out there," Franklin said. "I think we were right. He ran away on his boat."

"Did the snake follow him?" Billy asked.

"How the heck should I know? I thought you needed to pee."

Billy turned back and forth, then remembered where the bathroom was. He hurried inside and lifted the seat. Next came the sound of his stream hitting the pot.

Franklin gave another look at the riverside. Hope and dread raged on in an exhausting battle. He tried hard to hope his father was still alive, while fearing the worst.

In the time since the attack, he never questioned the absurdity of the existence of a giant snake. Yet, it did. He saw it with his own eyes. The only logic was that meteor storm that struck a few years back. According to the General who appeared on television, it was the cause for mutating everyday animals into giant monsters.

Even then, it still felt unbelievable. It was the fallacy of every human being. Never in a million years did he think it would ever happen to him. Things like this only happened to other people.

Yet, here he stood, anticipating the appearance of a man-eating snake.

"SNAKE!!!"

That one word and the horrific tone in which Billy screamed it, made Franklin sprint out to the front porch. Had it not been for that pesky conscience of his, he would've continued running to Mr. Tracy's cabin.

But he couldn't leave Billy behind.

Franklin turned around and hurried into the bathroom. In the two moments it took to get there, he expected to hear a smashing sound as the creature burst through the wall.

He turned the corner, ready to grab Billy by the shoulder. He found his little brother pressed against the wall, holding his pants up and catching his breath. At that moment, Franklin remembered there was no window in the bathroom, thus no way he would see the snake if it was outside.

Billy started to chuckle. He saw the confusion in his older brother's face, and tilted his head at the floor.

Franklin looked down. "Oh, geez."

Coiled by the plunger was a small garden snake.

Both kids stepped out into the hall, their hearts continuing to race. Billy took a seat on the living room sofa, then smiled.

"Sorry. I just saw a snake, and… well…"

Franklin smirked. "You thought it was going to eat you."

"Well, I, uh…" Billy's mouth slacked, his mind failing to come up with a convincing excuse to save face. Ultimately, it was better to go with the truth. He shrugged and smirked. "Yeah."

They laughed together, only to stand up to the sound of a vehicle engine approaching their driveway.

"That's not Dad's truck," Franklin said.

"Who is it, then?"

"Hopefully someone who can get us out of here. Let's find out."

The two boys ran out to the front porch.

CHAPTER 11

"So, it's all true? That meteor storm really caused all of this?"

Thomas could relate to the astonishment Hayden Spencer was currently feeling. It wasn't too long ago when he experienced it himself.

The exhausted civilian was wedged in the backseat between the Captain and Archer, the latter of whom kept a watchful eye on their surroundings while Charity drove them to the cabin.

"Unfortunately, it's our new reality," Thomas said.

"And you guys go around hunting them?" Hayden asked. It was more a statement than a question, for the answer was obvious. "The meteor storm happened in 2019. Have monsters been appearing all that time?"

"It took a while," Thomas said. "The first few appearances were fewer and farther in-between."

"They have been appearing in greater frequency as of late," Charity added.

Hayden nodded, still wrapping his mind over everything that had happened today. The fright from nearly getting eaten alive was not something one easily shook off.

He looked at Thomas. "So, you guys are part of a reconnaissance team."

"Correct," Thomas replied.

"You guys knew the snake was out here?"

"No," Thomas replied. "We were taking care of a completely different threat."

Hayden straightened in his seat, the veins in his neck bulging. "There's something else out here too?!"

"Another hornet colony," Thomas replied. "Don't worry, it's mostly taken care of. We have people taking care of the last remnants of them as we speak."

"We sent out a warning to all inhabitants in the area," Howard said. "But, even with all the technology at our disposal, we're still plagued by signal interference."

"That's why the gas station was closed," Hayden said. "Damn. The radio kept cutting out. I didn't receive the warning. My neighbor, Jack Tracy, didn't listen to the radio at all, and was the rare type that never carried a smartphone. Not that those get much signal out here either."

"A neighbor?" Thomas asked. "Where is he?"

"He's dead," Hayden replied. "Snake got him." Thomas nodded silently, his face hardening from the sense of failure. Hayden took a breath and, in an attempt to distract his mind, continued with his questions. He looked at Thomas. "So, you're the leader of this group."

"That's what they call me," Thomas replied.

"I'm guessing you all have different specialties. I guess yours is bossing people around."

Thomas chuckled. "I like to think there's more to it than that."

Hayden looked at Howard, seated in the front passenger seat. "What about you?"

"Engineer. Weapons and technology development. And chemistry," Howard replied, his eyes locked on his tablet screen.

"So, that flying drone that saved my ass was your invention. I guess I have you to thank."

This time, Howard looked up. "Thank you. Nice to know somebody thinks I do my job well." He glanced at Thomas briefly, then returned to monitoring the aerial feed from his drones.

Hayden shifted his gaze to Charity. "What about you? If he's a tech guy, I imagine you handle the biology side of things."

"You imagine correctly," Charity replied. "Biology, botany, geology, oceanography."

Hayden whistled. "What, are you guys like triple PhDs, or something?"

"We only hire the best of the best," Thomas said.

Hayden turned left to look at Archer. The sniper was looking out the window, rifle leaning against his lap.

"So, what's your specialty?"

Archer slowly turned his head, his indifferent expression unchanging.

"I shoot things."

Hayden nodded and shrugged. *Fair enough.*

He turned his attention to the trail. "We're almost there. Just follow this to the left."

Thomas noticed how the poor guy's foot was tapping incessantly against the floor. His hands were equally as jittery, their fingertips beating against his knees. Hayden was starting to breathe through his teeth.

The concern for his kids was front and center in his mind. For all he knew, the snake would beat them to the cabin. It had the advantage of mobility and an all-terrain physiology. The Growler was limited to the space of the few roadways and trails in the area.

Thomas put a hand on his shoulder. "Don't worry. We have another unit on the way. We'll have you and your boys to safety in a matter of minutes. What are their names?"

"Franklin is my oldest. He's twelve. And Billy is the youngest. Ten."

"Mr. Spencer, you have my word they will be protected," Thomas said. "Protecting human life is G.O.R.E. Sector's number one objective."

Hayden nodded. "Thank you, Captain. But if I may ask, why all the secrecy? What was there to gain by keeping knowledge of these mutations away from the public?"

The facial expressions on all four Raptor Pack members soured.

"Nothing to do with G.O.R.E. Sector, I promise you that," Charity said. "General Kilmore founded this organization strictly to find and exterminate these creatures. Unfortunately, we too had to be kept a secret, since our existence was linked directly to that of the mutations."

"To sum it up, there are powerful forces in the world, in government and in areas of influence, that want to weaponize these things," Thomas explained.

"And you guys don't agree with that?" Hayden asked.

Thomas looked him in the eye. "In the span of a day, I watched three colonies of insects invade an entire county. And that would've been just the start of that nightmare. Had they continued to procreate and form new nests, we literally would have been faced with an apocalyptic event. No, I do not agree with any foolish notion of weaponizing, or any other attempt to control these creatures. Once affected by the particles, they are no longer animals. They are monsters, hellbent on killing. The only cure is extermination."

Hayden remained silent. Though he sat still, there was a new aura of awareness in his eyes. Thomas knew that look. It was the sensation of having your world view changed. The way he figured it, the guy was grasping the full extent of the situation. *Or,* he had a change of opinion about something.

"You okay?"

"Yeah," Hayden replied. He chuckled nervously. "If I'm being honest, I guess I've had the wrong opinion of you guys. G.O.R.E. Sector, I mean. Since the news of

Ramsey County broke out, I thought you guys were just part of the coverup. Turns out, you're the ones who brought it into the light. Hell, I should be thanking you. You guys saved the world. Literally."

Thomas smiled. "My team did the hard work. I just pointed them in the right direction." He gave each of his team members a glance. "Without their expertise, all I would've known to do was spray bullets in the air and hope for the best."

Charity turned her head enough to see the Captain in her peripheral vision. Thomas could see a small, witty grin crease her cheek.

That's damn right, Captain. And don't you forget it.

"We're coming up on your cabin," she said.

They came up to the driveway, immediately seeing Hayden's pickup truck. The engine was still running. The cabin was fully intact, with no signs of damage.

Before the vehicle came to a stop, Hayden was reaching over Archer to open the door.

"Let me out. I gotta see if my kids are okay."

Thomas tapped him on the shoulder and pointed straight ahead. "All you gotta do is look." Hayden straightened in his seat and followed the Captain's finger. On the far left side of the porch were his two boys.

"Oh, thank God!"

Thomas stepped out and made way for the gratified father. Hayden ran to the porch and embraced his two sons. Howard, Archer, and Charity exited their vehicle and stood beside their leader, allowing the family their moment of reunification.

He took the opportunity to check in with Lieutenant Belanger.

"Guard One?" Thomas said into his radio. "We're at the cabin. What's your E.T.A.?"

"We found a crossway, Captain. We're almost there. Two minutes."

"Copy." He tucked the radio away and looked at Charity. She was smiling while witnessing the emotional reunification taking place on the front porch. "You good?"

"Oh, yes," she replied. "Just nice to have a reminder every now and then. Of why we do what we do, I mean."

Thomas gave thought to that statement. In his time in the military, he always heard phrases such as 'fighting for freedom' among others. But as the years went on, he doubted that was truly the case. Most military conflicts in the past few decades accomplished little more than enriching politicians and their donors.

But working for G.O.R.E. Sector was different. Here, he truly was making a positive difference. Seeing Hayden with his sons made him think of the larger picture. Every death of a G.O.R.E. Sector soldier or specialist was not in vain. They were not risking their lives for the Military Industrial Complex to have an excuse to build more bombs. They were protecting humanity. Sometimes as a whole. Sometimes, just one family at a time.

Every G.O.R.E. Sector soldier and specialist came into the job voluntarily. General Kilmore did not order anyone into this organization, for he knew the fatality rate would be relatively high.

It made Thomas reflect on his actions earlier at the hornet's nest. Indeed, Charity, Archer, and Howard were in a dangerous situation. And they would be again. And again. And again.

You can't eliminate the risk of danger, he told himself. Watching the Spencer family, he envisioned a world in which he failed delivering the cannisters into the hornet's nest. If he had, the swarm would have been out in full force, and this family would undoubtedly be dead.

Up on the porch, Hayden finally released Franklin and Billy from a suffocating hug.

"Dad, we thought it got you," Franklin said.

"Came a little close for comfort," Hayden replied, laughing. "How are you boys? You both alright? It didn't come back, did it?"

"No," Franklin said. "We hid in the cellar like you said."

"That's good. Thank you for listening."

"Dad!" Billy said, wiggling the sleeve of Hayden's shirt. "You're all wet."

Hayden stood up and observed his clothing. "Yeah. Wasn't quite a clean getaway." He turned around and gestured to the team members. "I suppose I should introduce you to the ones who saved my butt."

The boys took one look at Raptor Pack and felt their jaws drop. They had seen the patches on their sleeves a hundred times on the internet.

"It's them!" Billy shouted. "It's G.O.R.E. Sector."

"Holy…" Franklin looked at his father. "You found the G.O.R.E. Sector guys?! Dad, you're awesome!"

Hayden shrugged. He knew it didn't necessarily play out as intentionally as that, but he decided to relish in the moment all the same.

"Yeah. Sure."

"Did you watch them kill the snake?" Billy asked.

Hayden's newfound energy and enthusiasm quickly went away. "No. We need to pack our things and—" He noticed the way Billy was holding his arm. "What happened, son? Did you hurt yourself?"

"He fell and landed on it when we ran down the steps," Franklin said.

"How bad does it hurt?" Hayden asked.

Billy recoiled as his father touched the swollen area. "Hurts a lot."

Charity stepped forward. "I'll take a look at it. Howard, can you get the scanner?"

The engineering specialist was already on it. He reached into the storage area and grabbed a medical kit and a handheld scanning device.

"They'll get a look at it," Thomas told Hayden. "If it's broken, they'll probably have to set the bone before we buggy out."

"In that case, I'm gonna change my clothes real quick."

He hurried inside, leaving his sons with Charity. She took the equipment from Howard and walked with the boys to the bench on the front porch.

"Thanks for saving our dad," Billy said to her.

Charity nodded. "Don't mention it, bud. Don't worry, we'll get you to a safe place shortly. First, let's take a look at your arm."

In the meantime, Howard resumed monitoring the feed from his drones.

"How long can they stay in the air?" Thomas asked.

"They can remain in flight for twelve hours," Howard answered. "Assuming they don't get swatted out of the sky. They can descend down corridors, wells, other tight spaces."

The deuce-and-a-half engine of an FMTV rumbled in the distance. There was a crunch of vegetation and the scurrying of small critters as the large vehicle passed through the north trail.

It arrived on the front lawn and pulled over near the riverbed. Lieutenant Belanger and eight other soldiers streamed onto the grass.

"Go! Go! Secure a perimeter. Get seismic readers on every corner of the property line." He made eye contact with the Captain and walked over. "Sorry we took so long, sir. Not like there were street maps."

"It's fine, Lieutenant," Thomas said. "I'm not planning on being here long. Our target has proven to be unpredictable. Its location is presently unknown. Dr. Tate is searching the area with his drones, but so far, we have no clue where the bastard is."

"I'm working on it," Howard called out. "A lot of forest to cover, only two drones flying around. You do the math."

"The math will be having more drones available next time," Thomas said. "Maybe if you weren't too busy trying to build hundred-foot robots, you'd have more drones."

Howard shook his head. "Captain, if you knew how many advanced projects I have in development, you'd crap your pants. Be grateful, too."

"Grateful for crapping myself?" Thomas said. "No, thank you. I've got your cooking to thank for that."

"No, I…" Howard scowled. "First of all, that was not my fault. The store put out a recall for their ground beef the next day. Had I known beforehand, I would've never served you that batch of chili."

"Oh, sure. Blame it on the store," Thomas retorted. "Some chemist. Can cook up any recipe except edible ones."

"Hell of a victory celebration," Charity said under her breath. "Killed that giant fish in the Everglades with relative ease and no casualties, only for Howard to come along."

"I can hear you," the engineer barked. "And *secondly*, back to my initial point, you'll be grateful for MY MACHINES, because I guarantee you they will all come in handy at some point."

"How 'bout we start with those drones of yours," Thomas said. He and Belanger stepped onto the porch, tapping Howard on the shoulder as they passed by him. "Find that snake."

"Aye-aye, Cap."

Thomas was about to step inside when a thought suddenly hit him. He pivoted to face Howard.

"Hey, Doctor? You said you can maneuver those drones through tight spaces?"

"Absolutely."

"Without losing the signal?"

Howard shook his head. "Depends on the terrain, but in ground like this, they can travel depths up to seventy feet."

"Could you find the tunnel where it escaped and have one of your drones travel through it?"

Howard perked up. "Hmm! Why didn't I think of that?" Right away, he began manipulating his machines to travel downriver.

Thomas entered the cabin and admired the relaxing interior. Franklin was sitting on the couch, staying out of the way. "Not a bad spot for a getaway."

"Yeah," Belanger said. "Minus the killer man-eating snake." He gave a glance at the full pot of coffee on the kitchen counter. "Oh, nice. I don't suppose Mr. Spencer would mind if I stole a cup of this."

"Cups are in the upper cabinet," Franklin said. "Dad made that for the grizzlies."

Belanger froze, with one hand on the pot. "He... made coffee for grizzlies?"

"To keep them away," Franklin clarified. "They don't like the smell."

"Oh!" Belanger snorted. "That makes a lot more sense."

"Drink it fast, because we're heading out in the next minute," Thomas said. "Any word on the chopper squadron?"

"Last I heard, they were closing in on the princess," Belanger replied. "Shouldn't be too long now."

"Good. Once we have air support, we'll make short work of that snake," Thomas said.

"Wasn't it able to withstand explosives?" the Lieutenant asked.

"Explosive tipped bullets," Thomas said. "Rather low-yield. The snake survived, but the shots clearly hurt enough to make it want to retreat." He looked at the doorway as Charity stepped inside. "How's the boy?"

"Mid-forearm fracture. I made him a cast. He'll be fine," she said. "And to your point regarding the snake; yes, I agree. Its skin is thick, but I'm confident if we hit that thing with a steady barrage of hell-fire missiles, it'll be toast."

"Good." Thomas peeked out the window at the vast forest. "We've just got to find it first."

CHAPTER 12

Thomas stood beside Howard, watching the monitor as the drones located the large opening where the snake disappeared.

"Width is over six feet. Plenty of space," the engineer said. "Just so you know, this doesn't guarantee we'll find the snake. It could have surfaced anywhere."

"Still, it can give us a clue," Thomas replied.

"Can't argue with that," Howard said.

Lieutenant Belanger returned from a perimeter patrol, just in time to overhear their exchange.

"Hope we find it soon, because I'm already tired of this mother-effing snake in this mother-effing… forest?"

Three soldiers, Kove, Stewie, and Lent, hung their heads and groaned. As did Thomas.

"Yeah, um, permission to speak freely?" Kove asked. "I ask on behalf of Stewie here."

"Granted," Thomas said.

Kove elbowed Stewie. "You have a gift for words. Use it."

Stewie shrugged. "What can I say, gentlemen? We've seen our fair share of duds. Grenades, rockets… Lieutenant Belanger's one-liners. Perhaps it's a factory defect."

Lent snorted, then shifted into a strict position of attention when Belanger's eyes aimed his way.

"Yeah, yeah. You all can go to hell. But before you do, get the truck ready so we can get the civvies out of here."

"Aye-aye, Lieutenant," Kove said, not bothering to conceal his amusement.

Thomas glanced to his left to monitor Charity's progress with Billy's arm. Hayden stood nearby, wearing a fresh set of dry clothes. He had packed some essentials and was ready to evacuate.

"Ow!" the boy said. Despite his yelp, he forced himself to keep a stoic, 'tough' look on his face.

"Sorry, bud." Charity patted Billy's shoulder. "Almost done. Then we'll get you guys out of here."

Franklin took a seat beside his brother. "Think of it this way, Billy: when other kids ask you how you broke your arm, just tell them you helped G.O.R.E. Sector fight off a giant snake."

"Yeah, right," Billy said. "Like they would believe me. And besides, it doesn't change the truth. I hurt myself running away."

"And that was the right thing to do," Hayden added.

"Give it time, man," Thomas said to Billy. "I don't see this monster problem going away anytime soon. Once you're of military age, we'll be glad to have you on our team, if that's what you wish."

Billy smiled and looked at his brother. "That sounds cool."

"Dangerous…" Franklin said. It was an acknowledgement their father was pleased to hear. "But, honestly, I'd go for that too. I wish I didn't have to wait so long. Is there anything for kids? Like an army youth program, or something?"

"Yes, indeed there is," Thomas said. "There's the United States Cadet Corps. I can speak with General Kilmore and get you guys in. Or you could do the Civil Air Patrol. That's the weaker version… also known as the Air Force program."

With a snarky grin on her face, Charity raised a certain finger at him. "Sorry, kid. Don't repeat what you see here."

The boys laughed.

"It's okay," Billy said. "Dad often does it when he's driving."

"What?" Hayden exclaimed. "No I don't... Eh, who am I kidding? So, guys? You really interested in what Captain Rodney is proposing?"

Billy and Franklin looked at each other, as though to confirm with one another if they wanted to follow through on the idea. In unison, they gave their response.

"Heck yes." Hayden looked to Thomas. "I guess it's settled then. Thank you, Captain."

A feeling of warmth came over Thomas. "Pleasure's all mine." In that moment, he reverted back into business-mode and watched the monitor on Howard Tate's tablet.

The black screen now had the greenish tint of night vision. A circular scanning sequencer completed a cycle every few seconds. So far, it appeared the drone was alone in that tunnel.

"Damn snake traveled far," Howard said. "Even considering its size, I'm amazed it was able to tunnel underground at this distance. I imagine it has to be an exhausting process."

"Its ability to travel underground might make it tricky for us to concentrate fire on it," Charity said. "As you said earlier, we could kill it with a steady bombardment of hellfire missiles. But if it tunnels, we're back to square one."

"Based on what we've seen, it's quick to move underground if it's in danger," Thomas said. "If only we could trap the thing on solid granite where it couldn't burrow." As he spoke, he found himself staring at the mountain to the northwest. Much of its southeast side was barren. Rigid. "Charity? What do you make of the mountainside there?"

She laid the last touches on Billy's cast, then stood up for a better look. "Hard to say from here, but it looks like that bumpy section is made of rock."

"It is," Hayden said. He joined them on the far side of the porch. "You guys talking about that little ridge there? The one that almost looks like a shelf. Yeah, that's solid rock. Goes pretty deep, too. That snake might be strong, but unless it has a two-inch roller-cone bit on its nose, there's no way it's tunneling through that."

"Perfect," Thomas said.

"Yeah, perfect," Charity retorted. "Of course, there's the issue of getting a hundred-plus foot snake with a bad attitude onto that specific section of the mountainside. Aside from that, it's the ideal scenario."

"What's the matter, Doctor?" Thomas asked. "That sound like too much of a challenge for you?"

She put her hands on her hips. "I suppose we can figure out a way. Maybe devise a pheromone or something. But to do that, I need a DNA sample. You care to reach into its mouth and swab?"

Thomas recoiled from the thought.

"Sir?" Belanger called out. "Are the civilians ready for extraction?"

Thomas looked to Charity. "The boy all set?"

"Yep, he's ready."

Thomas gave a farewell smile to Hayden and his sons. "Go with the Lieutenant, gentlemen. We'll meet up later."

Hayden, Billy, and Franklin gave their thanks, then crossed the yard to the FMTV.

"Uh-oh."

Thomas and Charity spun toward Howard and his screen. The night vision was off. On the monitor was a forest.

"'Uh-oh'?" Thomas asked. "What's 'uh-oh'? I don't like 'uh-oh'."

Howard directed his drone up ahead a few meters. The scanning sequencer ran another cycle. The digital green circle settled on something in the distance.

The drone moved in on the object and brought it in view.

"Another tunnel," Charity said. "Looks pretty fresh."

"Go inside and follow it," Thomas said.

Howard steered the drone into the tunnel. A world of darkness eclipsed the screen, which reverted back to its night vision. It traveled for what felt like miles before they came to its exit.

The drone arrived in a patch of forest. It turned around and pointed its camera at a rushing river.

"Wait a minute," Thomas said. "That's the river. It was moving west. Howard, can you ascend and figure out where this is at?"

Howard elevated the drone. A world of branches assaulted their vision. Next, they saw a vast area of treetops with the river forming a long chasm in the green wilderness.

Two hundred meters southwest were a pair of clearings. He zoomed in on the southernmost one, seeing an FMTV, an M1161 Growler, a two-story cabin, and on its porch, his own face mouthing, "Oh, shit."

He zoomed out and focused on the tunnel exit. A trail of crushed vegetation led to the river. He moved it to the other side, finding a large groove in the mud. The trail angled to the south.

Straight toward the cabin.

By now, Archer was standing with his teammates, watching the images. All four members of Raptor Pack quickly connected the dots. This time, they shared a second, "oh shit."

Thomas looked at the FMTV. Lieutenant Belanger stood by the cab with five other troops and was waving for the Spencer family to come over.

"Lieutenant! Hold up!" he shouted. "We've got incoming from the north! Fall back to the—"

A crackling of tree branches interrupted the Captain. Wooden limbs swayed and leaves rained to Earth, unveiling the presence of the gargantuan reptile staring down at them.

"Oh, hell!" Lieutenant Belanger and his men pointed their rifles high at the reptilian monstrosity.

It had scaled the length of a large oak tree. Like a feline stalking an unsuspecting rodent, it was poised to strike. Its partially coiled body swiftly unwound, springing itself onto the yard. Immediately upon landing, it moved as fluidly as though skating on ice.

Gunfire shook the air, merging with a muddled frenzy of movement and commotion.

The snake raised its head like a cobra, twitching as its thick skin took a barrage of rifle fire. Most of its potential victims were backpedaling toward the cabin, with one tenacious soldier attempting to pull off a few shots from the rear of the vehicle.

He planted a few rounds near its already-injured left eye, both aggravating the snake and assisting in its selection process.

"Fall back!" Thomas repeated. Most of his men followed the order, save for the one trooper who now wished he did.

The snake struck. The soldier wailed briefly, his legs kicking as his upper half was shoved into its throat. A moment later, his heels were skyward. The snake parted its jaws and snapped shut again, piercing flesh with curved teeth. A lump rolled down its body, eventually disappearing somewhere in the middle.

Without hesitation, it slithered toward the porch, forcing the platoon to disperse. Thomas, Charity, and Howard planted several rounds on its neck, failing to do anything except annoy the creature.

"Get inside!" Thomas said to Hayden and the boys, who immediately obeyed that instruction. He looked to Archer. "You have those explosive bullets handy?"

Without saying a word, the sniper stepped forward and pointed his rifle at the snake.

He was immediately forced to take cover. After spotting Lieutenant Belanger and four other soldiers attempting to flank it from the west, the snake swung its body to counter. As it did, its tail lashed at Archer. Its tip came within a few inches of his face. In a flash of instinct, Archer raised the weapon as a shield.

Following a crack of metal, the sniper was knocked on his back. After a split-second moment of relief, he looked at the two halves of the specialized sniper rifle in his hands.

Like a freight train barreling straight out of hell, the creature closed in on the five soldiers.

"Look out!" Belanger shouted. With Kove, Stewie, and Lent on his six, he sprinted behind the cabin. The fifth soldier, stricken with panic, made a desperate attempt to climb into Raptor Pack's Growler.

The snake ceased its pursuit in favor of focusing on the sound of a revving engine. The soldier attempted to back the vehicle into the trail, only to feel the *THUD* of the tailgate hitting something sturdy and massive. That 'something' turned out to be the snake's midsection, after it had begun the process of looping itself around the vehicle.

In a matter of seconds, its body was pressing against all sides of the vehicle. There was a hiss of gas, a grinding in the engine, and the squealing of metal. The man in the driver's seat frantically looked back and forth. The sides of the vehicle were literally closing in around him.

By the time he realized what was happening, he was stuck. The driver's side door and the dashboard compressed against his waist and thighs. Shards of glass hit him as the windshield burst. The front and rear crumpled and folded upward, as did the flooring.

Thomas and the remaining soldiers continued raining gunfire on the creature, to no avail.

With one last scream that quickly turned into a long-winded croak, the soldier disappeared inside a teepee made of aluminum, steel, rubber, and plastic. Oil leaked from what was once the engine, mixing with gas from the ruptured fuel tank.

Archer was back on his feet. With no gun to shoot explosive rounds, he decided to use the next best thing: A simple grenade.

He pulled the pin, waited two seconds, and chucked it at the creature's head. Just like with every firearm, his aim was precise. The grenade burst right by the snake's jawline, spitting shrapnel in its face. Its head and neck lashed to the side, the tongue flailing from its gaping mouth as though it too was in anguish.

The creature uncoiled from the coffin, lashing Hayden's truck with the tip of its tail. A cloud of vapor burst from the seams of the hood. Rising steadily, the snake prepped for another strike, this time with intent to snatch the pesky Archer off the front lawn.

He already had a second grenade prepped.

It sailed through the air and struck the creature's throat right before exploding. The snake reeled backward, the rest of its body uncoiling and lashing into the driveway.

"Oh, sh—"

Private Stewie was knocked to the ground. He barely felt the impact by the tip of its tail. All he knew was that he was flying several feet backward and was now staring skyward.

Belanger, Lent, and Kove rushed to his side and got him to his feet.

Meanwhile, the snake, still flailing like a worm on a fishhook, continued to slash its tail like a kite in a heavy wind. Hayden's truck was struck again, its front tires bursting, the cab imploding.

"Howard!" Thomas said. "Get your drones over here. Get them to suicide bomb that bastard."

"You got it, Captain." Howard snatched his module and steered the two drones to the property. He typed in a short code, triggering a flashing alarm on the corner of his screen. *Explosives armed.* "Take a bite out of this."

"Everyone take cover," Thomas said.

Lieutenant Belanger and his team dragged the injured Stewie to the east side of the cabin.

Like a pair of thirsty mosquitoes, the drones zeroed in on the snake.

BOOM!

A tremendous shockwave rippled underneath the property. Bedroom windows shattered. Pieces of gravel and other debris peppered the west wall.

Thomas, stiffened by the shockwave, kept his eyes on the target. Though he was silent, his lips mouthed the words, "Please be dead."

The black cloud spiraled and thinned. Behind the gloomy curtain was a vertical, slender object with a pointed tip. Slowly, but truly, its length was slipping into the ground.

Despite the visual hindrance, it was clear what was happening.

"It's tunneling," he said.

The tail slipped under the earth, leaving nothing but a gaping hole in its wake.

CHAPTER 13

For a few moments, the team waited in silence, their weapons sweeping the ground. Slowly but truly, the adrenaline rush dissipated.

Howard swiped the monitor screen to bring up the readings from the seismic sensors. "It's still in the area. Readings are decreasing. It's moving off."

"Keep an eye on that reading," Thomas said. He started moving to inspect the ground where the snake was hit. "Charity, mind joining me?"

She puckered her brow. "Yeah, I kinda do in this instance." Groaning, she shouldered her weapon and pressed forward.

They crossed the driveway, stopping momentarily to glance at the wrecked vehicles. The Growler, and the rover inside of it, had been crushed beyond recognition. Most importantly, in that wreckage was the fifth casualty of the day.

Thomas gripped his weapon hard. It was the only strangling motion he could make.

Charity noticed his body language. "I know, Captain."

"It's part of the job, unfortunately," he replied in a forced, neutral tone. He didn't have to like it, but it was the truth.

They took a look at the battered tree line where the snake had tunneled. The ground was charred and ravaged, both by the explosions and the creature's writhing motions.

Thomas noticed something in the dirt. At first glance, it resembled a large fish scale. He picked it up and held it in the light.

"Piece of skin?"

Charity took it from his hand for a closer view. "Yep, it appears so." They both took a look at the ground, spotting a few more shavings.

"Got some blood over here," Thomas said.

Charity swallowed. With eyes wide, she hurried back to the porch.

"In that case, we're *really* in trouble. You know the rule about wounded animals, right?"

"They're twice as dangerous." With that in mind, Thomas was right behind her. He looked at Howard. "Is it still nearby?"

"To the northwest," Howard said. "Motions have slowed."

"Maybe it's dying," Lieutenant Balenger said. He stood beside Lent and Kove, who tended to Stewie.

"It better be," the injured soldier groaned.

"I wish," Charity replied. "The damn thing's just licking its wounds."

"Well good," Stewie said. "Gives me a chance to get even. That remark I heard you make about wounded animals being twice as deadly as before... just wait till that thing gets a load of me."

"How bad is he, Lieutenant?" Thomas asked.

"Few broken ribs," Belanger said. "He'll live, but we need to get him out of here."

"What are we waiting for? I say we get the hell out of here," another soldier said. Thomas glanced at his name tape. Johner.

"Private Johner, I promise we will. Except, we're down to one vehicle, and I'm not too keen on starting its engine at the moment."

"I agree," Charity said. "I have a feeling the snake will zero in on the vibration and attack. No freaking way we'll outrun it with that thing."

"So... what?" Howard asked. "It's obvious we can hurt it, but it burrows before we can inflict enough damage. Not that it matters anyway. Archer has no more explosive rounds. I'm out of C4. The thing can take a hell of a punch."

Thomas looked to the sky. "This is why I need my *entire* team." He snatched his radio. "Raptor Pack to General Kilmore. Can you relay a message to *Falcon* for me?"

CHAPTER 14

"Eagle Two and Three, guard the northwest ridge. One and Four, watch our six. Let's get this right because I *really* don't want to bore myself to death in another two-hour chase."

Renee was truly heartfelt in that last statement. The last two-plus hours had been nothing but a nonstop sweep of the Wyoming forests in search of the hornet princess and her cohorts.

It was bad enough that she was not the one to locate the princess. That achievement went to Eagle One. And knowing him, he would brag about it for at least a week. It was even worse considering she didn't believe the hornets would set up camp in this particular spot. They had chosen a small depression with a small lake on the northwest side and some large rock formations to the east and south.

She didn't consider it a prime spot for digging an underground nest. There would be a risk of flooding if they dug any tunnels too close to the lake, and in addition, the soil near the ravine was hard. Or so she thought.

Only now did she realize the upper layers were soft enough for them to dig. Once the bugs got down a few meters, they would be able to set up their nest under the rock formations. Ultimately, the bugs would have a steady water supply, thanks to the lake, and the best protection thanks to the rocks.

A large hole had already been formed in the depression. Every few moments, she would see one of the princess' escorts pop out, scooping dirt and gravel onto the outside. They wasted no time carving out their fortress.

"All units are in position," Eagle One said. *"How do you want to do this, Falcon? Bomb the hell out of it?"*

"That's tempting," Renee said. "However, if they survive the blasts, they could tunnel underground. We'd bury them alive and wouldn't know if they escaped until it was too late. If Drs. Black and Tate were here, we'd use their equipment to get a scan of the ground. But it's just us."

"Well, while you're deciding, should I go grab a coffee or something?"

Renee bit her lip. Eagle One could really be a smartass at times. It seemed to be a personality trait at G.O.R.E. Sector.

"If you do, grab me a pumpkin spice."

"They're not in season yet. It's still summer."

"Ugh! If people want me to keep saving the world, they better make it available all year round."

She stared at the nest for another moment, contemplating every available option.

Should've brought a couple of cannisters of Howard's pesticide. I guess I was certain we'd find those damn bugs mid-flight.

Every moment she wasted, the bugs were getting deeper. She knew she needed to act now.

The time crunch and an aggravating headache let to frustration, which in turn led to impatience.

"Screw it. Get your guns ready, boys. I'm knocking on the door." As soon as she spoke, she brought the *Falcon* a few meters above the next opening. She tilted the vehicle to a forty-five-degree angle, pointing the nose right at the opening.

"Oh, hell. I guess this is what happens when she doesn't get her pumpkin spice," Eagle One said.

"Damn right," Renee retorted. She blasted the forward machine guns. Two thousand rounds, measuring at 7.62x51mm, peppered the entrance and the inner walls.

Renee amped up the punishment for a count of twenty, then ceased fire. Sure enough, that did the trick.

The princess' three escorts scurried out of their incomplete nest. Wings vibrated, indicating a desire to set up house somewhere else. That, or they were just really pissed.

Last, but not least, came the princess. As Renee expected, she was an ugly creature. At the moment, she was twice the size of the others. Her claws and wings were caked with dirt, a consequence of squeezing herself into an enclosed underground chamber. She reared back on her hind legs, exposing her stinger. Her wings began to buzz, shaking the sediment loose before she could take flight.

Renee whistled an old country tune while she targeted the young colony. The computer flashed in red letters, *Missiles Armed.* She backed the *Falcon* up a couple hundred feet, then pressed her finger on the firing mechanism.

"Try shaking *this* off."

She unleashed her rockets.

In the blink of an eye, the four hornets disappeared behind a mountain of fire, smoke, and uprooted earth. Dirt and rock rained in all directions, the smoke climbing high into the sky.

Renee instructed her computer to perform a scan. What it found was a mess of insect parts scattered across the landscape.

"I think you got 'em," Eagle One said.

"What? You think I'd miss?"

"You did seem pretty shaken up about your favorite latte not being in season…"

"That is a tragedy that rivals the advent of a giant hornet invasion. I suppose I'll survive until September gets here." Renee switched channels to get in touch with General Kilmore. "Falcon One-Five to Boss Man. Got good news for ya. The runaway bride is now bird food."

"Perfect timing, Falcon," Kilmore replied. *"I just got word from Captain Rodney. He needs your help on the double."*

"Aw. You mean there's something he can't do himself," she joked.

"This is serious, Ensign. There's a new threat. Five soldiers are KIA. Looks like there's a giant snake in the area. It's killed at least two different households so far, in addition to our troops. According to your team, it is capable of moving underground, making combat rather difficult."

Renee immediately turned the *Falcon* to the west and gunned the engine. Her sense of humor vanished, replaced by a crushing concern for her friends.

"I'm on my way, sir." She switched channels. "Eagle Squadron, move your asses! We've got another player in the game."

CHAPTER 15

"Hang tight, Raptor Pack. Falcon and Eagle Squadron are on the way. Sure you don't want me to send additional ground troops?"

"Not unless you're trying to create more job openings, General," Thomas replied. "We're on the snake's turf. Ground troops and vehicles will create more victims. Our best bet is to hold out until the choppers get here, and we can airlift the civilians to safety."

"Copy that, Captain. Shouldn't be much longer."

"We'll be in touch." Thomas clipped his radio and faced the others. "At least there's some good news. Renee successfully killed the hornets."

"Thank God," Charity said. "I've had enough of bugs."

"As opposed to everything else we've dealt with?" Howard replied in a sardonic tone. "Like, I don't know, giant snakes?"

Thomas peeked inside the cabin to check on Hayden and his sons. Billy and Franklin were understandably nervous, having witnessed the recent attack by the snake. All things considered, they appeared to be handling themselves quite well.

"You kids doing okay?"

Billy gave a thumbs up. "Never better."

"So long as we don't get eaten," Franklin added.

"We'll see to it that doesn't happen," Thomas said.

Charity stepped alongside him. "Now that you've seen our work firsthand, I wouldn't blame you if you were having second thoughts about eventually joining G.O.R.E. Sector."

Franklin exhaled sharply. By now, he knew better than ever that this job was not fun and games. It was an important task that had high stakes. He kept his eyes on the floor, clearly giving her statement some consideration.

His eyes met hers. "No. I think, when I'm old enough, this is what I'd like to do."

"I still wanna do it," Billy said.

Thomas shared a glance with Charity. "Brave kids. I'm confident they'll do just fine." He turned his attention to Howard. "Any more readings?"

Howard shook his head. "Not for the last few minutes. Last reading was a hundred-fifty yards northwest."

The nervous soldier, Johner, stepped in front of the Captain. "Pardon me, sir, but maybe this is a good opportunity to get out of here. We still have the FMTV. There's enough room for all of us."

"Negative," Thomas said. "The thing knows we're here. I suspect it will attack if it senses us making a run for it."

The response got a sour look from Johner.

Lieutenant Belanger, noticing this, approached with an equally sour look of his own. "Soldier, whatever you're thinking about saying, double-think it, and then keep it to yourself. Nobody made you join G.O.R.E. Sector. Right off the bat, you were warned about the risks. Don't forget, you were brought in because you displayed talent and promise. Don't prove us wrong."

"I understand the risks," Johner replied. "It's a certain somebody's judgment I'm not too fond of. I'm not eager to get killed because I was ordered to stand around."

Howard stood up, holding his module at his side, his stare penetrating deep into Johner's soul. "Kid, the Captain's not making this order willy-nilly. He's trying to keep you *alive.*" He paused momentarily, reflecting on his own words. "Regardless of whether the call is right or wrong, there's something to be appreciated in that."

"Absolutely," Charity added.

Johner, feeling outnumbered, silently backed away.

It was moments like this where Raptor Pack was reminded everybody made mistakes and poor judgments. In this case, it was the G.O.R.E. Sector recruits who hired Johner out of the Army. Clearly, he was not among the best of the best.

This fact was proven by his next action.

"Suit yourself."

He turned on his heel and sprinted for the FMTV. Being the driver, he had the keys in hand.

"Kid, don't!" Thomas shouted.

Belanger raced onto the porch, pointing a finger. "I'm gonna have your ass!"

Johner got into the FMTV and started the engine, which came alive with a mighty rumble. He brought the vehicle forward and angled it to turn into the trail.

"Oh, shit!" Howard stammered. Without specifying to the rest of his team, he quickly grabbed his radio. "Johner. Get out of the vehicle now. The Captain was right. It's COMING!"

In that moment, Thomas, Charity, and Archer caught a glimpse of the seismic readings on his monitor. The snake was on the warpath.

An explosion of dirt prefaced its appearance. The FMTV came to a sudden halt. Dirt, grass, and roots smothered its windshield. It reversed, the driver not only blinded by the dirt, but also his own panic, unaware that he was speeding right for the river.

Not that it made a difference.

The snake towered from the earth, its neck scabbed in places. It arched its neck to gaze at the large vehicle. As though weighing no more than a typical garden snake, the creature launched itself the rest of the way out of the hole.

Its jaws closed over the right side of the engine. Its hundred-and-thirty feet of body length quickly sealed around the front of the FMTV.

Johner opened the door, only for it to immediately latch. It bent inward, the leathery body on the other side pressing with increasing force. The engine ruptured and the front tires burst. Windshield glass cracked, then burst into fragments.

"Now! Now!" Thomas shouted. "Get out through the windshield!"

"Hurry it up, you idiot!" Belanger shouted.

Johner, seeing the cab literally closing in around him, climbed through the only opening. He cleared the gap, nearly getting caught between two loops in the snake's body. Boots touched grass and carried him toward the cabin. His career may be over, but perhaps he could manage to keep his life.

With one final squeeze, the snake crumpled the vehicle. It raised its head, spotting the human retreating to the structure. Like a line coming off a fishing reel, its body uncoiled from the heap of metal that used to be the FMTV and glided across the lawn.

"Inside! Inside! Everyone get inside!" Thomas ordered. This time, there was no questioning his orders. Especially not from Johner.

Thomas was the last to enter the cabin. He slammed the door shut and, going by basic instinct, slid the lock home. In the following moment, he could sense his team members staring at him.

Their thoughts could be summed up in one word.

Really?

Thomas looked at the small metal lock, then shrugged.

"Yeah, I know."

A moment later, the snake proved their unspoken point. A single impact broke the door into a dozen fragments, all of which came flying into the living room.

The snake's head squeezed through the door frame, chipping its edges.

Thomas, having just cleared his vision after getting hit in the face by a door fragment, gasped as he saw the dark-skinned, triangular snout coming straight at him.

He hit it point blank right between the eyes with his carbine. The impact only spurred the creature further. Thomas was rammed by its snout. All of a sudden, he was on his back and in a daze.

"Shoot it!" Belanger shouted.

The Spencer family pressed their hands to their ears as several rifles cracked inside the cabin. Multiple impacts chipped at the skin, successfully distracting the creature from its target. It whipped its head side to side, knocking over Lieutenant Balenger and another soldier, before turning its attention back to the Captain. It parted its jaws, revealing the dark red interior of a long, narrow throat.

From the left came Archer. In his hand was a Desert Eagle loaded with fifty-caliber bullets.

BANG!

Blood jetted from the snake's right eye. Hissing with a decibel level rivaling the gunfire, it whipped its head to its right, knocking Archer into the kitchen. It retracted its head through the doorway and began circling the cabin.

Charity took Thomas' hand and helped him to his feet. "You alright?"

"I'm good, thank you."

"Eh-hem!!!"

Charity looked to Archer, who was getting up off the floor. "I was gonna check on you next."

"On that note, everyone alright? Hayden? Boys? You hanging in there?"

Hayden was pale in the face. To everyone's amazement, the boys seemed to be holding up pretty well, all things considered.

"This is the wildest trip we've ever been on," Franklin said. "What do you think, Dad?"

Hayden looked his oldest son in the eye. "Next trip's gonna be at the beach. Far from the woods."

He shivered as the snake brushed against the south wall.

Howard Tate stood in the hallway, sensing the vibrations. "I don't know what it's up to, but I already don't like it." Soon enough, they could hear a grazing sound on the east wall. He stepped back. "I really don't like it…"

HISS!!!

"GEEZ!!!" He sprang a full six feet, then turned around and pointed his gun toward the bathroom. On the floor was a small garden snake, now slithering back into the farthest corner of the room. He lowered his weapon and chuckled nervously. "I thought… well…"

"I know that feeling," Billy remarked.

After seeing the creature glide past the front window, Thomas instructed everyone to gather near the hall. Two of the soldiers stood at the rear, guarding the south entrance. Thomas remained in the living room, watching the creature as it strangely appeared to come to a stop near the window.

He could see its tail through the doorway, which was pointed eastward, while the snake's head was pointing west.

"Charity? Is it doing what I think it's doing?"

Before she could answer, the cabin began to shake.

"Yep. It's trying to constrict this entire cabin," she said.

"With us inside it!" Howard exclaimed.

Thomas reflected on the cabin his team had found earlier in the day. It was approximately the same size as the building he stood in right now. Judging by the aftermath, the snake had little problem crushing that place. By that logic, this cabin was doomed.

"We're in a bit of a pickle."

Belanger called to the men in the back. "Gentlemen, can you get that door open?"

One of the soldiers tried opening the back door, only for the snake's body to dent it inward. A split-second later, the entire back wall began to crack.

"No go, sir."

The window near the kitchen began to crack. The ceiling fan shook, with cracks forming around its base.

"Raptor Pack, this would be a perfect time to come up with some whacky, outside-the-box idea," Belanger said.

Thomas peeked out the kitchen window at the Growler. "Damn it."

"What?" Charity said.

"Howard had a rover in there. It held a cannister of the pesticide. I was hoping we could shoot it from here and maybe jettison its contents, and maybe drive the snake away with the chemical cloud. But I can't see it from here."

Now Franklin and Billy were getting nervous. They huddled close to their dad.

"Too bad it's not a grizzly," Franklin stuttered. "Dad could just brew a bunch of coffee."

Charity's face came alive. It was the look of somebody having a major lightbulb moment—A look Thomas was very welcoming of in the moment.

"Tell me you have an idea."

She dashed into the kitchen. "A crazy one... though I guess for us, crazy is fairly normal."

"Crazy is fine, as long as it works," Thomas said. He noticed how she was opening the cabinets and inspecting the contents. He connected that with Franklin's recent statement about the coffee. "Are snakes sensitive to certain household odors?"

"A bunch of stuff. Lime, vinegar, hot pepper, garlic, some oils. I just need to figure out where all the stuff is. I'm a field girl. Kitchen work is not my forte."

Franklin and Billy shot to their feet.

"We know where the stuff is," Franklin said.

"Mom was a heck of a cook," Billy added.

They ran into the kitchen and checked the cabinet on the left. Billy climbed onto the countertop and dug for the ingredients Charity mentioned. Franklin grabbed a large skillet from under the sink and placed it on the stovetop.

Howard joined the makeshift operation. "Make way. I'm the chemist here. Boys, are there onions or anything in the fridge?"

Franklin dug out a pair of onions and a jar of minced garlic. "Oh, look! Dad was smart enough to grab some lime juice too."

Hayden watched with astonishment and admiration. "Y-yeah. Totally was planning on fending off a monster snake attack when I bought that."

Billy passed down some salt, pepper, vegetable oil, and cinnamon.

Howard filled the skillet with the oil and began adding the salt and pepper. Franklin went to work chopping the onions, just as his mom had taught him in the past. In years past, he considered it a chore. Now, he couldn't be more grateful for the skill.

"Watch out." He scraped the contents into the skillet. An angry broiling sound growled.

Howard turned the heat to maximum, filling the kitchen with a spicy odor. He added the cinnamon, lime juice, and the entire jar of garlic.

Meanwhile, the snake tightened its grasp. The east wall took new form, its center bending inward. The cracks in the ceiling enlarged, dropping the living room fan onto the floor. All four blades burst into pieces. Glass cracked and shattered, leaving a massive opening where the living room window had been.

The snake raised its head and quickly peered inside with its one functioning eye, as though to gauge the status of its victims.

"Hey guys?" Belanger said. "You know, I'd hate to rush you, but…"

"Shh!" Thomas interrupted. "Let them work their magic."

Howard resembled a master chef as he stirred the recipe with a wooden spoon.

"You know? This could use a little extra kick. Archer? Could you get me some gunpowder, please?"

The sniper removed a few bullets from one of his magazines, then removed the gunpowder from them. Following Howard's gestures, he went ahead and dropped the contents straight into the recipe.

WHOOSH!

By now, the smoke was filling the entire cabin. The gaps in the doorway and window worked in the team's favor. Wafts of smoke, carrying a repulsive odor, made their way to the snake's nostrils.

It flicked its tongue repeatedly, clearly put off by the strange smell. As a response, it tightened its grasp, crunching the south, east, and north side of the cabin.

The west wall, where Howard performed his cooking, began to shudder and crackle.

"More veggie oil," he said, spilling the rest of the bottle into the skillet. He dumped the remainder of the cinnamon and black pepper.

More and more smoke billowed from the sizzling mixture.

"Ah-ha!" Billy said. "I found the vinegar." He passed a large jug over to Howard.

"Now this is what I'm talking about!" He added the contents.

The smoking intensified.

By now, everyone else was gathered in the hall to get as far away from the suffocating fumes as possible.

The snake appeared to shift in place. Its head rose and fell, bashing the porch like a massive hammer on plywood. A forked tongue flicked nonstop. As the moments passed, the snake was entombed by a greyish-black cloud.

Finally, it couldn't take it anymore. It released the cabin and raced north across the yard.

Thomas rushed to the window, waving his hand to clear himself of the fog. He saw the tip of the snake's tail disappear into the hole at the northern edge of the yard.

He found Howard's module and looked over the seismic readings. The snake had moved a bit to the west and was now heading south, positioning itself behind the cabin.

The rest of his team worked on fanning the smoke out of the cabin.

"Nice work, everyone," Thomas said. "That drove the bastard away. We can just hang here until Renee arrives."

"Oooooh, hell! I don't think that idea's gonna work out, sir." Howard switched off the burner and tossed the scalding hot skillet outside. He pulled the stove a few inches away from the wall and shined a flashlight behind it.

By now, the smell reached Thomas' nose. "Oh, you've got to be kidding me." "Yeah, we're leaking gas," Howard said. "Must've ruptured when the wall started caving in."

"Can we switch it off?" Charity asked.

"The meter's behind the cabin," Hayden said. "I mean, if you reeeeeally want to go out there, I won't stop you."

The thought made her cringe. With the cloud drifting into the front yard, there was nothing repelling the snake from the rear.

"It's not too far away," Thomas said. "It's waiting."

"What's the plan, sir?" Belanger said. "Wait and hope Eagle Squadron gets here in time?"

Charity waved a hand in front of her nose. "Don't think that's feasible. I'm already getting light-headed. And God forbid that thing attacks. Even a muzzle flash could grill us all."

"We have to move," Thomas said. "Mr. Spencer, how far is your neighbor's property?"

"In walking distance," Hayden said. "If we sprint, we can get there in no time. Though… we'd be ripe for the taking."

"We can improve our odds by creating a decoy of some sort. I don't suppose you have a four-wheeler or something so we can distract the snake?"

Hayden shook his head. "Had a boat, but that's gone."

Thomas moved to the middle of the living room. "Is there a television or a radio we can blast in the basement? All we need is to distract the snake just for a few moments, give us a head start."

Franklin jogged to the sofa and picked up his Nintendo Switch. "Would this work?" He put the volume on max and played the menu screen for his current game.

Billy found his and did the same.

"Yeah, that should do the trick," Charity said. "If we get them in the cellar, the vibrations might be enough to get the snake's attention."

"Only one way to find out," Thomas said. "Everybody get ready to run."

CHAPTER 16

The beast was not ready to quit yet.

It was blind in one eye and repulsed by the humans' nauseating odor. Unlike the rest of the forest's ecosystem, they were not simple creatures. They were complex and organized, utilizing unique defense mechanisms.

But they were still organisms, as easily digestible as the largest grizzly. The snake, motivated by intense hunger and an inexplicable desire to kill, took a moment to rest.

Curled twelve feet underground, it listened to the movement coming from the habitat, hoping one would exit out the back. For a small amount of time, it sounded as though they chose to wait in the large chamber where the fumes emitted from. In that time, it pressed its eye into the dirt, jampacking the wound. In time, the eye would heel. Despite the injury, the creature was more than capable of eliminating all remaining humans in the structure. It just needed the opportunity to present itself.

Before long, it appeared that opportunity had arisen. New vibrations caught its attention. These were the same as the others. Footsteps. But much deeper. The habitat must've had a subterranean aspect to it.

The repulsive fumes were probably not present in this underground chamber, meaning anything in there was nearly defenseless. It knew it could ram through the walls with relative ease, even with the earth impeding its momentum.

More vibrations reached its sensory receptors. These were surface level, moving north. Footsteps—*many* of them. The group was fleeing.

At the same time, the subterranean noise intensified. The snake could not identify what was occurring, but whatever the sound was, it was definitely manmade.

It chose to go after the nearest target.

Spearing through the earth, the snake homed in on the underground chamber. Like a battering ram, it smashed through the artificial barrier. Now in an open space, it pointed its snout at the source of the noise and prepared to strike.

Except, nothing was present.

It flicked its tongue and turned its head to search with its good eye. The sound was coming from a pair of objects on the floor. The tips of its tongue touched one of the noisy items, instantly confirming it was inedible.

Pushing its way up the steps, the snake emerged in the habitat's ground level. All of the humans were gone. Judging by their vibrations, they were heading north.

The snake had no conscious realization that it had been tricked. It had no ego, nor did it feel a need for payback. Just an endless yearning to kill; a byproduct of the mutation instilled by the extraterrestrial particles.

***

"I think the plan worked," Charity said.

Thomas stopped near the front door of Jack Tracy's cabin and looked to the south. The sounds of the snake crashing through Hayden's cabin could not be mistaken.

Right in the nick of time, Renee's voice came through the radio.

"Falcon to Raptor Pack. You guys still alive?"

"'Bout damn time you showed up," Thomas responded. "What took you so long? Get outsmarted by some bugs?"

"Oh, you're hilarious," Renee said.

Eagle One gleefully chimed in. *"Actually she did! I found the princess in an area Falcon thought was impractical."*

"Thanks, Eagle One."

"How far out are you?" Thomas asked.

"Fifteen miles. We'll be there in a couple of minutes."

"Couple of minutes is a long time, Captain," Charity said. She glanced again to the Spencers' cabin.

Thomas could hear the same thing she did. There was a grinding of dirt, meaning the snake was tunneling under the patch of woods between the properties. Any minute now, it would emerge from under their feet.

"That it is." Thomas was staring at the dock. Moored to it was a sixteen-foot motorboat. Inside was just enough space for the Hayden family and the remainder of Belanger's squad.

Time was not on his side. A decision had to be made now.

"Lieutenant."

"Yes sir," Belanger said.

"Take your men and get Hayden and his sons on that boat. Go north as fast as you can."

"What about you, sir?" Belanger asked.

"My team and I will stay here. We'll hold its attention while you guys get some distance. One of the choppers will intercept you and airlift you to safety." Thomas pointed to Stewie. "Mind letting Archer have your weapon, soldier?"

Stewie passed his carbine to the sniper. "Pop that snake's other eye out for me." Archer winked in response.

Belanger helped the injured soldier to the boat. "Not like you're gonna need it anyway. Serves you right for all those remarks about my one-liners."

"Make a good one, and I'll finally say something nice," Stewie groaned.

"Yeah, right," Belanger said. "Come on, boys! You heard the Captain. Get to the boat. On the double. Move it! There's a hungry snake heading this way."

Hayden stepped in front of the Captain, all at once remorseful and appreciative. "Sir, you can't stay behind. You could get killed."

"That's part of the job, Mr. Spencer," Thomas said. "The important thing is that *you* are not killed. Now, please, go with the Lieutenant."

Hayden opened his mouth to argue, but held back. He understood what the Captain was saying. He offered a quick salute. It was sloppy and crooked, but Thomas appreciated it all the same.

The following moment, he was aboard Jack Tracy's boat. His sons and the rest of the team were crammed on its deck, with Belanger at the motor. It came alive at the first pull, and despite the weight it carried, backed out effortlessly.

Raptor Pack gathered inside the cabin. It was a nice place that was kept neat and organized by its late owner. All in all, it was a smaller structure than Hayden's cabin, with the kitchen and living room being one area, and only a few feet of hallway leading to the back. To the left was a set of stairs leading to the top floor where the bedrooms were located.

"Here we are at the bottom of the ninth," Thomas said. "Howard, are your seismic readers picking up anything?"

Howard took a look at his module. With his face scrunched, he turned his eyes back to Thomas.

"Yep."

They all felt the vibration under their feet.

Floorboards burst up to the ceiling as though blasted by an air compressor. Like the tentacle of a mythical kraken, the snake emerged in the middle of the living room, its head punching a hole in the ceiling.

Howard staggered backward and fell against the stairway. The snake tore its face out of the gash it made in the ceiling and bared down on him. Dirt was caked against its right eye, which was deflated and saggy. It flicked its tongue once, then moved in for the kill.

Archer, always executing his timing perfectly, threw himself in its path and thrust his rifle outward—right as those jaws parted. The impact knocked him backward and would have guaranteed his demise, had he not squeezed the trigger in that moment. Several rounds tore into the back of the snake's throat.

In a single, destructive motion, it yanked its head back and tore through the front window.

Now outside, the creature began circling the cabin.

"Upstairs!" Thomas said.

They ascended to the second floor. Charity glanced out the master bedroom window.

"Here we go again," she said.

A booming *crunch* and a violent shake revealed the snake was repeating its strategy of constricting the cabin. With the building being smaller, it was able to wrap its body more effectively.

The cabin shook again. Then again. The floor shifted, making Thomas question the decision to move upstairs.

"Renee! Your two minutes are up!" he radioed.

"Like a wizard, I'm never late, nor am I early. I arrive precisely when I need to. Now, look out your window."

Thomas did just that.

Like a flock of geese in a triangular formation, Eagle Squadron followed *Falcon One-Five's* lead.

At two hundred yards, they held position while she moved in closer.

***

"Whoa!" Renee exclaimed. No amount of experience fighting mutations could have prepped her for the sight of a giant snake crushing a building as though it was a rodent. "What's that thing trying to do, Captain? Give you a hug?"

"I've had enough affection for one day. Get the thing off of us, will ya?"

"I'll see what I can do. I mean, I could blast the thing with rockets, but then G.O.R.E. Sector would have to hire a new research-reconnaissance team."

"You were bragging about being like a wizard a second ago," Thomas said. *"Turn it to stone, or something."*

"Not sure about that," Renee said. "But, I'll try for something a little more practical. I'd get to the other side of the cabin if I were you." She activated her forward guns and targeted the snake's hide. "Let's see if this works."

A stream of bullets struck the creature. It hissed and loosened its grasp. In a corkscrew motion, it climbed the cabin and positioned itself on the roof, its tail twitching against the east wall as though it were a rattlesnake. It was looking at her now, visibly incensed and eager to retaliate.

"Ohhh, it's pissed."

"So am I," Thomas said. *"It's been a long day. Any chance we can speed this up before we get crushed?"*

"Sorry, Cap. I shot the thing a bunch of times. Its skin is pretty damn strong. I could try chasing it off of you. Maybe if I got it on the ground, Eagle Squadron and I can blast the thing."

"It'll dive underground," Charity said. *"We need to get it on the rocky side of the mountain. There, we can throw everything we have at the thing without it escaping."*

Renee looked at the mountain and laughed. "Oh, right! And how do you expect me to get it there? Book a bus ticket?"

The moments of silence sparked greater tension than the presence of a giant snake. Knowing Thomas Rodney, he was coming up with a preposterous idea, and it would be up to her to pull it off.

"No, but how 'bout a flight ticket?"

She felt the blood drain from her face. "Beg your pardon?"

"How much weight can the Falcon hold?"

Renee leaned forward as though to shout at him through the window. "Are you for real? You expect me to *fly* the snake to the mountainside?"

"You've got an ejection seat."

"Oh! I feel so much better. You know these aircraft are expensive, right?" Another few moments of quiet increased her angst. No doubt the Captain was gearing up to aggravate her with an intricately strung choice of words.

Instead, what she got was much different.

"It's our only chance at killing this thing, Ensign. Only you can do it. If you don't, it'll get away and more people will die."

There was an unspoken part of that message she took in. Captain Thomas Rodney was not seeking a path of low-risk, as he had done that morning. He was trusting her to pull off a very risky tactic that could very well end her life.

He had accepted the full magnitude of being a leader.

A moment later, he followed up with an aggravating string of words designed to grate her nerves.

"Alright. Fine. Maybe Eagle One can pull this off. Or I can get someone from the Canadian Air Force."

The blood returned to her face, turning it beet red.

"Oh, you did not just go there!"

"I did. What are you going to do about it?"

Renee bit her lip. "I have half a thought of letting the thing eat you, but Charity might yell at me, so... FINE! You owe me a pumpkin spice if I survive this."

"No problem," Thomas said. *"The café in town was advertising them."*

"Wait a sec, WHAT?! Eagle One, were you aware of this?"

"No comment, ma'am."

"Ooooh!" Now truly incensed, Renee sped the *Falcon* straight at the snake. It snapped its jaws a few times, unsure if it wanted to commit to a full strike. Renee turned the vehicle to the side, keeping the rotors as far from it as possible. "Come on. Take a bite."

She banked to port, bumping its head against the hull.

Now, the snake was ready to commit. Shaking its tail with rage, it rocked its head back, then threw itself at the *Falcon*.

The aircraft jerked to the right, then dipped a few feet as thousands of pounds of snake lashed underneath it. The creature wrapped its tail over the starboard side and over the top, steadily securing a firm grasp in which to crush its metal enemy.

"Passenger is fastened! Off we go!"

She pointed the cockpit northwest and accelerated to a hundred-fifty miles per hour. The snake proceeded to loop itself around the middle of the aircraft, its body managing to stay under the rotors.

The mountain grew larger and larger, the bumpy details of the rocky section becoming increasingly distinct.

Eagle Squadron was right behind her.

"Don't wait much longer, Falcon. Looks like the thing's starting to squeeze."

Alarms flashed in the cockpit. She looked over her shoulder into the fuselage, right as the sides began closing in.

"Oh, really? I couldn't tell!'"

She instructed the autopilot to fly straight into the mountain. The usual confirmation requests came in, which she had to acknowledge.

She was now at five hundred yards. Four hundred. Three hundred.

A pull of the lever ripped the roof of the cockpit free and launched her skyward. The *Falcon* passed underneath her, the snake still clinging to it.

Two hundred yards.

One hundred.

BOOM!

Her parachute deployed. Rocking back and forth, Renee watched the fifteenth model of her signature aircraft plow into Tusk Mountain. Every explosive armament detonated, resulting in a gargantuan fireball. In its center was the thrashing head and tail of a colossal snake whose flesh was threatening to peel from its body.

***

Thomas and his teammates assembled at the end of Jack Tracy's dock. From there, they had a good view of the mountainside. All at once, they flinched at the sight of the blast, unsure of the fate of their companion.

"Eagle One, please tell me she got out," Thomas said.

"I got a visual on her parachute, Captain."

Raptor Pack let out a collective sigh of relief.

From behind them came the sound of an engine. A Humvee passed through the trail and pulled into the yard. The passenger door opened and out stepped General Kilmore.

He marched directly to Raptor Pack. "A little more than we bargained for, wouldn't you say, Captain?"

"Nothing my team couldn't handle, sir," Thomas said.

"Indeed." General Kilmore took a look at the blast through long-range binoculars. "Snake is so big, I can actually see it from this distance." He passed the glasses to Thomas.

Through them, he could see the snake attempting to burrow into the mountain. As he predicted, the rock prevented its escape.

"Now it's time to see it in pieces."

"Couldn't agree more." Kilmore lifted his radio. "Eagle Squadron, finish it off."

A barrage of missiles spat from the helicopters and pummeled the snake.

It took several minutes for the smoke to clear. When it did, Eagle Squadron confirmed the completion of Thomas' wish.

The snake had been blown to pieces.

***

A high-pitched whistle signified Lieutenant Belanger's satisfaction. Aiming the boat to a clear patch of shoreline, he watched the enormous cloud of smoke climb high into the atmosphere.

"They did it," Hayden Spencer said. He hugged Billy and Franklin tightly. "I love you guys."

"Love you too, Dad," they said.

Belanger smiled at that, then resumed watching the fiery aftermath.

"That's how you end with a 'banger'." He looked at Stewie, anticipating a sardonic reaction.

Stewie shared a glance with Lent and Kove, then shrugged.

"You're improving," he said. He wiggled his hand. "But that's like saying you're serving rabbit shit for dinner instead of dog vomit."

Belanger pursed his lips.
"Tough crowd."

CHAPTER 17

Thomas' wish had been granted. It was lunchtime, and all of the mutations in the area had been eliminated. Granted, it was true only by a technicality; it was a late lunch. But as the popular saying went:

"Better late than never." Thomas lifted his burger as though to raise a toast. They stood at the hilltop where General Kilmore oversaw the operation against the hornets. A local diner in a nearby town had been generous enough to donate lunch for the men and women of G.O.R.E. Sector, which was delivered by helicopter thanks to the local police force.

Most importantly, they were kind enough to deliver a pumpkin spice latte for Renee Larson.

"Indeed," she said. She wore a big smile on her face.

General Kilmore joined Raptor Pack at the command post. "Another one in the books. Well done, everybody."

Thomas picked up a beer and raised it in a genuine toast. "To our fallen. May they rest in peace."

Charity, Howard, and Archer did the same with their beers.

"And to Eagle One and his exquisite work in locating the hornet princess," Howard said. The team watched Renee's souring facial expression and laughed.

"He gets one more hour to brag about that," she said, finally cracking a grin. "That being said, *I* was the one who blasted that wench out of existence."

Thomas grinned at the pilot's attempt to save face. "I guess we'll need a *Falcon-One-Six* soon, won't ya?"

"Part of the job," Renee said.

"On that note…" General Kilmore glanced at Howard. "Dr. Tate? Would you agree it's time for Lieutenant Larson to upgrade?"

Renee cleared her throat. "Lieutenant?"

"Seems appropriate," Kilmore said. "Unless you object."

"Hell no! And what's this upgrade? You got a new bird for me to fly? Please say yes."

"Oh, yes," Howard said.

"A new invention?" Thomas asked. "You're not referencing a super robot, are you?"

Howard moved to Renee's side with his module. "Ignore them." He brought up a 3D image of his designs for her new advanced aircraft.

"Now we're talking!" She faced it toward the rest of her teammates. On the screen was a machine that almost resembled a mechanical insect. Instead of rotors, it relied on a variety of thrusters. In addition to numerous rocket cells and machine guns, it was equipped with laser technology. "I love it. What's it called?"

"Eh. I tried a few names. They all sucked. I decided it was best not to overcomplicate it, so I settled on MEAV."

Renee frowned at the uninspired word. "MEAV?"

"Mm-hmm. Monster-Eliminating-Aerial-Vehicle."

Renee was smiling again. "Perfect."

"Congratulations, Lieutenant," Thomas said. He turned to face the General. "The Spencer family back in town?"

Kilmore nodded. "The local PD gave them a ride on their chopper. I hear you promised to speak to me on their behalf, though."

"Those kids were real troopers. We'd be lucky to have them when the time comes. Hopefully they'll still be interested."

"I have a feeling they will be," Kilmore said. "You guys do more than protect the public with your lives.

You provide hope and inspiration to people. Call me sentimental, but I think the world could use more of that." He grabbed a beer out of the cooler and raised his own toast. "This one's for you guys."

No way was Raptor Pack going to deny themselves their moment. They raised their drinks and accepted the General's praise. Then it was bottoms up.

"Aaaahhh!" Kilmore placed his beer on the table and grabbed a folded stack of papers from his back pocket. He placed it on the table, revealing a map marked with red X's."

"Oh, great," Charity said.

Kilmore grabbed a burger. "While we're here, we might as well go over the next assignment."

Renee shrugged. "As usual. No rest for the weary."

"Gather around," Thomas said. Raptor Pack assembled on Kilmore's side of the table, munching away while they studied the map. As usual, those X's meant trouble. "What have we got, sir?"

THE END.

Made in the USA
Middletown, DE
25 March 2025

73271010R00090